URGE

BETH YARNALL

URGE

ebook ISBN: 9781940811932

print ISBN: 9781940811550

I dedicate this book—the hardest book I've ever written—to the authors of The Keeper Shelf who have supported me in numerous, varied, and profoundly necessary ways. You are my New York.

And to my husband, Mr. Y, for buying into and supporting every single one of my crazy Lucy and Ethel schemes... including the one where I thought I could write a book.

1

There weren't a great many things that bothered Erin December. For the most part, she considered herself a pretty even-keeled person. So why was her face hot and the back of her throat aching with the words she couldn't let loose? As she sat in the Kavender Investments staff meeting, listening to Ramie Kavender heap praise on Austin for the success of the Petrie project, she couldn't believe what she was hearing. That son of a bitch Austin accepted the compliments as if they were his due, never once daring to glance her direction or acknowledge that she had any part in the project, let alone admitting she had done the bulk of the work.

She reminded herself that she was grateful for the job. The tiny town of San Rey, in central California, had been hit hard by the downturn in the economy. Kavender Investments was one of the few companies thriving amongst speculation of another recession. Without this job, she might be forced to leave the town she grew up in and move to a bigger town like Santa Barbara or Los Angeles. She liked her job and most of the people she worked with. She was confident in her work in a way she'd never been in any other position she'd ever held.

But that didn't mean she liked being stepped on by Austin on his way to a higher title.

As soon as the meeting was over, she escaped to the relative quiet of her cubicle. She pulled up the report she'd been working on before the meeting began and started to recheck the data one last time before she turned it in. A shadow fell over her.

"I have a favor to ask," her boss Ramie said.

She turned in her chair.

"Chelsea went home sick. She had a Cash for Keys appointment this afternoon at four. Can you take it? Should be quick. You can go straight home from there."

That was in half an hour and she still had the report to finish. "Sure."

"Thanks. I owe you one." He dropped the folder on the top of her already teetering stack and strode away.

She suppressed a sigh and reached for the file. The tab had the name Lasiter on it. She knew a Greg Lasiter from high school. Opening the file, she confirmed that it was *the* Greg Lasiter she'd be meeting with. Great. Just great. He was an asshole back then and while he didn't waste time picking on her anymore, he wasn't exactly nice.

The words in the file blurred, then blacked over. Her body seemed to shoot back as though she were on a rollercoaster, pain searing between her eyes. The sensation made her stomach dip. She knew what this was. She hadn't experienced this loss of control since she'd first come into her ability when she was eight. Shoved suddenly from one reality into another against her will, she found herself standing on the front porch of the Lasiter house. She worked to steady her breathing. Leaves danced across the lawn, the wind whipping them up, then sending them scattering.

What was happening?

She hadn't called up this vision. She hadn't chosen to be here in this time or this place. Trying to get her bearings, she glanced back at the neighborhood she'd walked through once upon a time on her way to and from elementary school. The street was empty.

She never used her ability. Ever. Only her Aunt Cerie and her father, Donald, knew what she could do. She kept it that way on purpose, holding her secret inside since the night her mother had left and never came back.

In the vision she was herself, knocking on the door of the Lasiter house, calling out for Greg. No answer. She pushed the doorbell and rapped on the door again. Silence. She shuddered from a chill she couldn't feel. Something was off.

Not real, she reminded herself. Her body still sat at her desk, but her mind had traveled through time. Was this the past or future? Why was she here? *How* did she get here? What did this loss of control over her ability mean?

Turning the knob, she expected it to be locked, but

it turned easily. She walked into an empty living room, stripped of furniture or anything that made it a home.

"Greg?" she heard herself call out. "It's Erin December from Kavender Investments. Hello? Anyone here?"

A light around a door at the end of the living room drew her attention. Her steps weighted, she found she couldn't stop. Any of it. Not her body from moving forward nor her mind from staying in the vision. She was stuck. Left with no choice. She closed her eyes, using the tools she'd been taught to search for a way out. But there was no ending it. The shock of that radiated through her. This had never happened before either. She'd *always* been able to pull out of a vision.

She put a hand out and opened the door. It swung away, revealing a small kitchen. Greg lay on the floor face up, a pool of blood around him.

He was dead.

She gasped and stumbled back.

As abruptly as she was sucked into the vision, she was spit right back out. She dragged in air, gripping the edge of her desk. *It wasn't real. It wasn't real.*

The file still lay open on her desk. The office seemed to go on about its business around her, oblivious to what she'd just gone through. She pulled her phone out to call her aunt to tell her what had happened and saw the time. A quarter to four. She had fifteen minutes to get to Greg's house. Greg. She should call for someone to save him. She punched in 9-1 then hesitated, her thumb hovering over the second one.

What would she say? Who would believe her if she told them what she'd seen in her vision?

She wasn't supposed to use her ability to change the future. That lesson had been drummed into her at an early age, from the first flickers of her ability asserting itself. If she changed one thing, it could potentially change a thousand little things. A man was dead. Or would be dead. Certainly there were exceptions. But wouldn't saving him be the absolute worst-case scenario? Could she live with herself if she did nothing? What choice was there?

She put on her coat and grabbed her purse and the Lasiter file. There was something wrong with her ability for sure. It was out of whack, totally out of her control. Maybe it wasn't true. Maybe her vision was wrong. *Please let it be wrong.*

She pushed through the door of the building where Kavender Investments had offices and onto Main Street. The people of San Rey went about their day. She envied them. She'd never wanted her ability, never wanted to be marked as different. She'd only ever wanted to fit in. Born into a family that didn't hide who they were, Erin felt like an outcast there too, keeping her ability a secret and never using it. She passed through town, attracting her usual amount of odd stares and whispers. She was used to it, but today she challenged their stares, glaring back when she would've glanced away.

Greg couldn't be dead.

Quickening her pace, she kept an eye on the sky, which seemed to increase its threat of rain with every step she took. It was the kind of sky her superstitious Aunt Cerie called volcanic, a portent of violence. Erin didn't subscribe to her aunt's superstitions, but she certainly wished she hadn't left her umbrella in her car, and her car with her aunt. That's what Erin got for loaning it to Cerie and for wearing suede heels on a day with a forty percent chance of rain.

Couldn't she catch a break just once?

She gripped the leather handle of her bag tighter as she broke into a jog, hoping to get to the house before the sky opened up. Not that she was in any hurry to get there. She passed homes, some vacant, some close enough that they'd taken on the same hollowed out look. The economic downturn had hit San Rey especially hard.

She opened the front gate of Greg Lasiter's house, releasing the leaves stuck to it, and slowly made her way up the front walk. At the door, she hesitated and prepared herself for the reality of the images that had assailed her when she'd touched the property file. A simple Cash for Keys, Ramie had said.

But nothing was ever simple in Erin's world.

Taking a deep breath, she knocked. If her vision were true, no one would answer. *Please let Greg answer.* Brushing the shards of flaked gate paint from her fingers, she was tempted to just pull out her cell phone and place the call she'd started at the office. But that's not how it worked. If her vision was real, the scene had to play out exactly as she'd seen it.

Clutching her bag tighter under her arm, she

knocked again. "Hello? Mr. Lasiter? It's Erin from Kavender Investments."

She felt stupid calling him Mr. Lasiter instead of Greg. He was only a year older than she was. She'd had a stupid unrequited crush on him her freshman year of high school. And now she was standing on his dilapidated porch, supposedly waiting for him to open the door so she could take the keys to his home. The home he'd grown up in. She shouldn't feel guilty about that and yet she did.

"Mr. Lasiter?" She rapped on the door again. "Hello?"

Inside, the house was silent. Outside, the only sound was the whoosh of wind, lifting the curling ends of her brown hair, bringing with it the briny tinge of the ocean and a chill that bit right through her wool coat. Just like her vision. If Erin was smart she'd follow her instincts and run back the way she'd come. But she had her father's practicality and a bank balance that didn't allow for fear.

She had to see this through.

Still no answer. She'd hoped so hard that what she'd seen would be as wrong as the way it had come to her. She closed her eyes and silently chanted the words of protection she'd been taught as a child, mentally drawing a shield around herself. Focusing her energy, she took three deep breaths, letting each of them out slowly, preparing herself for the possible reality of what she'd only seen in her mind.

She opened her eyes and turned the knob. Locked. She hadn't expected that. Her visions *never* wavered.

For a moment, she didn't know what to do. The wrongness poked at her.

Careful what you wish for.

Maybe there was a key. She searched the usual places—under the doormat, above the door, the light fixture, a dead potted plant—there.

Dusting the dirt from the key, she revealed a floral pattern. It was one of those novelty keys Fine's Hardware had started carrying some time back. Erin had one herself. She dug her key ring from her pocket and compared the near identical house keys. The irony wasn't lost on her. If it wasn't for her job with Kavender Investments, Austin or Ramie himself might have knocked on her door with a check to exchange for the key to *her* house.

She pocketed her keys once again and fit the dirt-smudged key from the planter into the lock. It fit, turning easily in the knob. The door creaked on rusty hinges, the curse of coastal living.

"Hello? Mr. Lasiter?" Her voice echoed off the walls of the near empty room.

Daylight made a weak effort to invade the space, casting no shadows. It was colder here, but not cold enough to mist her breath. The air lay still and ripe with wariness, as though the house had not yet made up its mind to accept her. Or maybe she was the one who refused to accept what had been so clear in her vision. She didn't want to go into the house, didn't want to be the one to make the discovery.

The layout was different from what she'd seen in her mind. Almost a mirror image, except for a door where there should have been a hall, and a fireplace where there should've been none. The differences were disorienting. It took her a moment to get her bearings. Different. Everything was so *different* from what she'd seen.

Why? What does it mean?

She called out for Greg again. No answer. She should leave. Right now. But her feet propelled her farther into the room as if controlled by someone or something else.

She swallowed at the lump of dread in her throat. She'd been drawn to the door at the far end of the room just like her vision and now there, standing before it, she couldn't seem to stop her shaking hand from reaching out to open it. A noise from the other side made her flinch.

She swung the door open slowly, revealing the room inches at a time. "Greg? It's me, Erin, fr—" She let go of the knob, clamping both hands to her mouth. The door continued on its own, exposing the scene.

Greg knelt over the body of a woman sprawled out on the floor in a thin pool of blood.

Behind him, the kitchen wall was dotted and streaked with more blood. He slowly raised his gaze. "I didn't do it." He swayed back and forth. His eyes, dull with shock, stayed on Erin's. "I didn't do it."

Erin lowered her hands, resting them over her pounding heart. This wasn't right. None of this was right. Greg was the one who was supposed to be dead. "Who... who is she?"

He looked back at the woman, squinting down at

her as though he was trying to figure that out. "Deidre," he finally answered. "My wife."

She knew that. *Didn't she?* Yes, Deidre. She'd met her a few times. But it was supposed to be Greg lying on the floor. "Wh... what happened?"

He stood and held out his hand to Erin, watching her now as though she had the answers to her own questions. That's when she noticed the gun resting in his bloodied palm. She started, knocking a shoulder into the doorframe behind her. They stared at each other across the kitchen. Thin beams of light filtered through the blinds, slashing everything in the room. The air was thicker here, so thick she could barely breathe, her chest heaving with the effort. The raw scent of blood and death filled her lungs, making her nauseous.

"I didn't do it," he insisted again.

"O-okay."

"You don't believe me."

"I do."

She'd answered too quickly. His eyes widened a fraction and then he looked around wildly as though searching for a way out. His fingers flexed over the gun, drawing her attention to it. She reached for the doorframe, needing its solidity. Her vision tunneled on the weapon.

The feeling of being sucked back, then jerked out of her body and dropped into another time made her clutch for the wall that wasn't there. She saw Deidre, whole and well, here, sitting at the kitchen table. She was waiting for someone, a neat stack of paperwork in front of her. She'd dressed carefully, her makeup just so. Something important was about to happen. Erin could feel Deidre's excitement. At a knock on the back door, Deidre stood, smoothing out her skirt. She opened the door, smiling.

A gun was thrust at Deidre, forcing her to move back into the room. Deidre gasped, her hands going to her mouth. Sunlight crowned the head of the person holding the gun, shrouding his identity. Erin could feel Deidre's shock turn to confusion, then fear. The same fear burned in Erin's chest. This was someone Deidre had loved and he'd come to kill her. Erin stared at the gun as Deidre did and then the room exploded in blinding light.

"I didn't do it!" Greg wailed, plunging Erin back into the here and now. He swung the gun in a wild arc. "I didn't do it!"

She sucked in air. Real and not real blurred for a moment. *What was happening?*

"I know you didn't," she answered, placing a hand over her stomach, trying to staunch the nausea.

She was sure Greg hadn't done this. Even though the murderer's identity hadn't been revealed to her through Deidre, Erin was sure it wasn't Greg. The clothes, the body type, and overall sense of the person were very different from the image she'd seen in her vision. Her vision couldn't be wrong a second time. *Could it?* She shook her head rejecting that thought.

Greg looked down at his wife as if noticing her for the first time. His face contorted, his eyes clamped tight. His hands went to his head. The gun thumped dully against his skull. "No one's going to believe me."

"I believe you."

"Why did they kill her?" he sobbed, dropping to the floor. His knees dipped in his wife's blood. "Why... Why... Why...?" He smoothed a hand over Deidre's face and hair, smudging them red. The light in the room changed with the waning daylight, bathing them gray.

His grief over his wife's death filled the room, pouring from him into Erin. Her chest ached with it. This wasn't right. None of this was right. *Why?* Why her? She wasn't made for this, didn't have the capacity to deal with...dear God...murder. This was *murder,* not the suicide she'd seen.

They needed help. Erin pulled her cell phone from her purse, her hand shaking so bad that she almost dropped it. "We need to call 9-1-1."

"No! You can't. You can't."

"Please, Greg. We need help."

"Don't." He came up kneeling, his hands clasped over his chest. "They won't believe me. They'll think I did it."

"Greg..."

Tears lined his face, falling in fat drops like the rain just beginning outside. "She was going to leave me." He sank back down on his haunches. Deidre stared blankly at the ceiling as her husband caressed her once again. "I don't blame you, baby. I was an asshole. I can't believe you stayed as long as you did. God, you're so beautiful. What am I going to do without you?"

Erin spoke quietly into her phone, her heart

beating so hard she could hardly get the words out. "Can you send the sheriff to—"

Greg whipped his head toward her, jerking back as if she'd slapped him.

"—321 Amiable Lane."

Erin recognized the police dispatcher's voice. Mabel Johnson was a lot of things, including a good friend of her aunt's, but discreet wasn't one of them. Erin would set the phone tree ablaze with her next words.

"There's been a...murder."

"A murder!" Mabel exclaimed.

Erin could hear Jessica, the sheriff's secretary, in the background, rushing over to where Mabel sat at the dispatcher's desk. "Who's murdered?" Jessica asked Mabel.

"I don't know yet," Mabel told Jessica. "Let me ask Erin. Erin, honey, who's been murdered?"

Erin didn't like the glee in Mabel's voice or the fact that Jessica probably had her ear pressed to Mabel's so she could hear everything Erin said.

Erin's gaze fell to the woman on the floor. She was so young. "Deidre Lasiter."

Greg stood, glaring at her as though she'd betrayed him, the gun balanced in his shaky palm. She'd managed to keep the panic from her voice, but it made her lightheaded and sick.

"Are you sure she's dead, honey?"

"Yes." Erin wanted to scream. "Can you please just send the sheriff?" She punched the off button on her phone and shoved it into her coat pocket, trying to hide her trembling hands.

"You shouldn't have done that," Greg said, inching closer.

"I'm sorry. I-I had to."

"Deidre's killer will go free."

"It's going to be all right."

"No, it's not! You don't get it." His eyes held wild violence, like the sky churning and spitting outside. He put the barrel of the gun to his head and cocked it. Snot dripped down his lips and chin. "All you Decembers are supposed to be some kind of fucking clairvoyants, aren't you?"

"No. Not me."

"Did you predict this?"

Shaking her head, she put her palms up. "No, Greg. Don't. Please don't."

He held her gaze for a moment and then he closed his eyes.

"Noooo!"

He pulled the trigger. Blood shot out, splattering everywhere. Erin knocked into the doorframe behind her. Greg crashed to the floor next to his wife. His blood mixed with hers. A fine red mist covered Erin from head to toe. She gasped for air—her head reeling—and almost dropped to her hands and knees. Righting herself, she scampered backwards. Into the living room with its grayed walls and orphaned furniture. To the porch with its pumpkins that no one would carve. Over the walk to the rotting gate. And out onto the deserted sidewalk.

Lightning flashed overhead. Rain pelted as if a thousand accusing fingers poked at her, each one blaming. She lurched into the street and turned to look at the house. It glared back with its black-windowed eyes and fat, picketed mouth. It, too, condemned her. She should have seen this. *Why hadn't she seen this?* Her chest heaved, her skin prickling in the cold damp air. In the distance, a siren wailed over the pounding of the rain.

The house blurred and she swiped at her eyes. Pink tinged water mixed with the black of mascara on her hands. The shaking started with a jolt. She wrapped her arms around herself to control it. *Greg.* Bile bubbled at the back of her throat until she bent over and let it all out, heaving into the cracks in the pavement.

She wiped her mouth with her sleeve, stumbled over to the curb, and dropped onto the wet cement. The trembling wouldn't stop. *Why didn't I see this?* She slammed her fists on her thighs. Damn it! Why had the vision been so wrong? What could she have done differently?

The sheriff's patrol car slammed to a halt in front of 321 Amiable Lane. She watched him climb out and look around. A second patrol car screeched to a stop at the curb, then another and another. San Rey's entire police force had shown up. This was big news. There hadn't been a murder in this town since 1943 when one brother had accidentally run over his twin, knocking him into a ditch where he'd hit his head and died.

The sheriff directed his men to search the property, guns drawn. Three went to the back while the sheriff picked two more to go with him through the front. The leftover few stood around, looking at each other like they'd just won the lottery. Moments later, the sheriff came back out and scanned the street. His gaze halted on Erin sitting on the curb across the street. She stood up, careful to avoid the mess she'd made. Shoulders hunched against the downpour, she retraced her steps to the house.

The closer she came to Sheriff Graham Doran, the deeper his frown grew. She came even with him, then just stood there, not knowing what to do or say.

"*You* called it in?" he asked, taking in her appearance.

"Yeah."

"Don't you have an umbrella?"

She looked up at his curt tone into eyes a shade or two bluer than the blackened sky. He was annoyed with her, and not hiding it. What was wrong with him? What had she done to irritate him?

"Sorry." She was on the verge of crying, but she'd be damned if she'd cry in front of him.

He made a rough noise at the back of his throat, then stomped off toward his cruiser, muttering under his breath. He came back with an umbrella, popped it open and thrust it at her.

She frowned. "I'm already soaked."

He folded his arms over his chest. Rain dripped off the bill of his sheriff insignia baseball cap into the space between them. He wasn't the sheriff his father had been, opting for a more casual look than his father's brass-buttoned jacket and flat-rimmed Mountie hat.

"Why did you come here?" he demanded.

"To do my job."

"Yeah, I'd heard Cadaver Investments was circling Greg's house. Come to pick the bones clean?"

She pulled in a breath. "It's *Kavender* Investments and I came here to give Greg a check. We had an appointment."

"Oh, I'm sure you did." He looked around at the other empty houses. "You've had a lot of appointments in this neighborhood already."

"My company has, yes. It's what we do."

"You came here to take the man's house away from him right after he lost his job and his wife left him. You're doing God's work, for sure."

She knew his anger wasn't directed at her specifically. Greg had been his friend and a reminder of what might have been his fate, had he stayed. Her job sucked. So did his. Seeing Greg like that shook her and she couldn't stand the man. She could only imagine how Graham felt.

She knew all that and yet his words still stung. "We all have our jobs to do even if we don't like them."

He inclined his head toward the house. "Just give me the brief on what happened in there."

She looked back at the house and the flashing rage Graham had ignited dulled to a simmering roar. The other officers had all gone inside, no doubt so they would have something to tell folks over breakfast tomorrow down at The Do or Dine Diner. She closed her eyes on the images that flashed across her mind of Deidre and Greg lying on the kitchen floor. If only she could scrub it from her memory.

Opening her eyes, she turned to Graham. "I went into the house, looking for Greg—"

"You just waltzed in."

"No. I found a key in the pot by the door. Kavender owns this house now. I had every right to go in as their agent."

"Right. So you went in, then what?"

She couldn't tell him about her vision. She'd been so careful, keeping her ability a secret all these years. Even so, she knew there was something about her that marked her as different, something that set her apart. It was more than her quirky aunt and her motherlessness. She made people uneasy, their gazes connecting briefly, then skittering away. They didn't stand too close to her or draw her into idle conversations. Maybe it was something inherent like some kind of silent signal, making them wary of her. She didn't know. She'd spent too long trying to overcome whatever it was, to no avail. Revealing her secret wouldn't change anything.

"When I walked into the kitchen, Greg was standing over Deidre with a gun in his hand." Erin exhaled hard. "She was dead."

"He was alive when you arrived?"

"Yes."

"Then what?"

"He was upset. He said he didn't kill her."

"They all say that."

"Yeah, but I really don't think he did it."

His posture changed subtlety, shifting toward her. "Go on."

"He kept saying that the police wouldn't believe

him. I told him that I believed him. He started crying and knelt down... he, ah..." She paused, not knowing where to look, tears brimming her eyes.

Graham moved closer, dropping his voice to where only she could hear him under the umbrella. "You're doing fine. Go on." His nearness brought back old memories and the thousands of times she'd wished for him to get this close.

"Greg knelt down beside her, his knees in her...in her blood. And he stroked her hair. It was kind of sweet. He told her he loved her and that she was right to leave him. He apologized."

"For what?"

"Everything. I guess. He was saying goodbye to his wife. I think he really loved her."

"What did you do?"

"I called 9-1-1. He didn't want me to. But we needed help. He kept saying that no one would believe he didn't kill her. And then he...he...he put the gun to his head."

Graham made a move to pat her shoulder, but pulled the gesture last minute. There was something in his gaze, something unguarded and searching. "I'm sorry."

Glancing at the house, she shrugged and crossed her arms over her chest. She didn't let herself think about how much she *wanted* his comfort, his arms around her, holding her. Having him back in San Rey after all these years... She shook her head. She couldn't let those thoughts get any further. They'd never be what she wanted them to be.

A sky blue 1955 Cadillac Fleetwood rolled to a stop at the curb next to Graham's cruiser. A burl of a man unfolded from the driver's seat and plunked a gray fedora on his head. Ham Doran still carried himself like the sheriff even though his son had replaced him. He adjusted the collar of his raincoat, nodded at Graham, then turned toward the house. There was a jerk in his stride as his gaze snagged on Erin, but he quickly covered and continued on into the house.

She followed Ham's movements until he disappeared inside, unable to pull her gaze away from the old sheriff. His dislike for her family ran deeper than her memories. As many times as she questioned her father and aunt about it, the harsher their reaction to her inquiry became until she stopped asking altogether. Whatever had happened between Ham Doran and her family would stay a secret.

"Shit," Graham grumbled.

"Looks like someone forgot to tell your dad he's not sheriff anymore," Erin said.

"He's not supposed to be straining himself. I'm going to have to take a baseball bat to his damn police radio."

"Old habits are hard to break."

"Maybe." He frowned at her. If he knew how badly the fullness of his lips ruined the expression, he probably wouldn't bother with it. Drops of rain dotted his beard and Erin tried to remember what he looked like without it. Was it soft? What would it feel like on her skin?

"Look," he said, breaking into her thoughts and

eyeing the new cars driving up the street. Mabel had obviously spread the word. "You're covered in evidence and you need to come to the station to make a formal statement."

Erin glanced down at her rain and blood soaked coat. Sparring with Graham had distracted her. Maybe he'd intended that by baiting her about her job, but his words brought back the horror of the situation. She was literally covered in pieces of Greg. Her mouth filled with saliva. She pulled in sharp, cold air through her nose, trying to quell her queasy stomach. He watched her, no doubt taking in the fact that she was barely holding on. She managed a brief nod.

"I'll need to take your clothes in as evidence. Do you have any others you can change into?"

"Not with me, but I can have my aunt bring me some. You really have to take my clothes?"

More cars arrived and people began to set up tailgate-style, with lawn chairs and Easy-up tents. Ice chests were opened, beers passed and one enterprising voyeur set up a Hibachi grill. Greg and Deidre's deaths would be the event of the century and no one wanted to miss it. She liked a great many things about the town she grew up in. But sometimes—like now—the smallness of it suffocated her.

Graham looked a little sorry for her and a lot pissed off at their audience. "Let's get you in the car. I've got to get this crime scene secured." He took the umbrella and held it up as he guided her to his car. He covered her as she climbed into the backseat of the cruiser, then leaned in. "Don't talk to anyone. No phone calls, nothing. Got it? I'll be right back."

She nodded and he closed the door. He didn't look back at her as he made his way into the house. She leaned against the hard, molded plastic seat and closed her eyes. The shaking started again, this time a combination of cold, fear, and being too damn close to Graham Doran.

2

Graham had seen some shit in his days on the LAPD, but nothing as dismal as the sight of his old high school buddy lying in a pool of blood, bits of the left side of his head floating in his wife's blood.

No—there'd been one worse.

The one he couldn't talk or think about.

He pushed those thoughts aside and tried to focus on the scene before him.

He and Greg had double-dated at their senior prom and played on the football team together. He didn't recognize the woman Erin had said was Greg's wife, but then he hadn't seen Greg much since Graham had left for the police academy in Los Angeles.

He hadn't seen much of anyone from San Rey and had preferred it that way. In the weeks since he'd come back, at least temporarily, he'd run into everyone everywhere. He couldn't turn around in this godforsaken small town without bumping into his first grade teacher, his old pediatrician, the girl he lost his virginity with. Or Erin December.

He hated seeing Erin like that, pale and afraid. The gore she'd witnessed... He'd known hardened police officers who couldn't handle what she'd seen. Hell, two of San Rey's finest had already lost their lunches in the bushes outside the house. He'd pushed her buttons trying to stop her shivering. It had worked. She'd taken the bait and damned if she hadn't warmed him up, too.

She'd changed a lot since the last time he'd seen her. Or maybe it was him who had changed. In any case, *something* had changed, making him take note of little things about her like the way her eyes sparked when challenged and the small mole near the corner of her mouth that drew his attention to her lips. Once he'd noticed it, he'd had a hard time looking away and not imagining what it would be like to kiss her. Totally inappropriate thoughts at a thoroughly inappropriate time, but there they were. They'd taken root and he doubted he'd be able to still them or keep them from following completely inappropriate paths.

"The coroner and crime techs are on their way over from San Luis Obispo," Paxton Riggs said, his voice muffled by the hand he had over his mouth, no doubt to block the stench of death. "Might take them awhile to get here with this weather."

Pax should've been elected sheriff. Instead he'd been overlooked in favor of Ham Doran's son. Small town politics. Pax was older and had been a deputy longer. Graham expected him to be bitter. Instead he got something completely unexpected from Pax—respect and acceptance.

Pax leaned over the woman's body, his shoes millimeters from the edge of the blood pool, his face going a couple shades paler. "Murder/suicide, ya think?"

"We don't get to decide. We collect evidence," Graham replied. He could see how it could've gone down that way though. The difficult thing would be determining whether or not Erin's version of events matched the evidence or if they told a different story altogether. Graham turned to two other sheriff deputies who looked greener than the wallpaper behind them. "Wrap the yard in police tape and keep the crowd to the other side of the street. And whatever you do, don't talk to them. I don't care if they're your sister, your wife or your mother. Got it?"

They mumbled their yes sir's and practically ran outside.

"Dexter, I want you to stand at the door and keep the log. Everyone who comes inside the house signs it. When the Crime Scene team and Coroner get here, they'll sign it. Station yourself on the porch. I want a tight record on this one."

Dexter bobbed his head, clearly grateful to be far away from the kitchen. "Yes, sir."

Graham turned back to Pax who was doing a good job of holding himself together. "Make sure the team tests both victims' hands for gunshot residue, then have them come over to the station when they're done with the house. I have a witness whose clothes will also have to be tested."

"Erin December? What'd she say happened?"

"She said the woman was already dead when she got here and that Gre— Mr. Lasiter killed himself in front of her."

"Rough."

"Where's my pop?"

Pax jabbed a thumb over his shoulder, his gaze glued to the couple on the floor. "Out back looking for clues. He noticed the backdoor was ajar when we got here."

"Damn it." Graham started for the door. "Don't touch anything and get those other guys out of here. Send a couple of them out to knock on doors. I want to know if anyone left in this neighborhood saw or heard anything. I want the rest of the deputies outside, protecting the scene. Anyone who was off duty is officially on."

"Don't be too tough on your old man. It's been hard on him, giving up his job."

"I know."

He did know. Pop had taken the loss of his job hard. Seeing his once strong, able-bodied father angry and frustrated by the betrayal of his body was difficult. Ham had always been larger than life, filling up the room with his presence. The shrunken, defeated man who came home from the hospital just a few short weeks ago was nearly unrecognizable.

Graham found his father studying a spot on the ground near the back of the garage. "If Mom knew you were here, she'd kill me."

Ham glanced up. "So don't tell her." He looked older in the dying light, thinner, frailer.

"I'm sure she, like half the town, already knows." He came up alongside his dad and stared down at the ground. "Find something?"

"Nah. Just trying to get a picture in my head of what happened." Ham shoved his hands into the pockets of his trench coat. "Greg was a friend of yours, right?" He continued without waiting for a response. "Heard he'd been through some tough times lately, losing his job and such. Heard his house had been bought up by that new investment company—Calendar something or other."

"Kavender Investments."

"Right. Right. I take it that's why that December girl was here."

"Her company bought Greg's house. She came here to make sure he'd moved out." And found a hell of a lot more than she'd bargained for. Graham frowned over that.

"She say what happened?"

"Only that Mrs. Lasiter was dead when she got here. Why don't we go in, get out of this rain?"

"Sure. Sure." Ham led the way to the little covered back porch. He stopped on the top step, peering through the window at the scene in the kitchen. "Murder/suicide. What a shame."

"Who says it's murder/suicide?"

"From the looks of it, is all. But then I'm guessing you've seen more of this than I have."

"More than I should have."

"Some might tease that you brought it with you from L.A." Ham reached for the doorknob.

"Don't! Damn it, Pop. You shouldn't touch anything without gloves on. You shouldn't even be here."

Ham snatched his hand away. He quickly cloaked his hurt in anger, drawing up to his full size, which wasn't as intimidating as it used to be. "I may be just a country cop to you, but there were never any murder/suicides on *my* watch."

"Pop, I—"

"Stuff it." Leaning in, Ham lowered his voice. "I know what you think of me, of this town. Five generations of Dorans have been sheriff here." He jabbed a finger at his chest, right over the heart that had cost him his job, his health. "That means something to me." He poked his son in the chest, over his healthy heart. "And it should mean something to you, too."

"I never said it didn't."

"You didn't have to. It's written all over you." He looked pointedly at Graham's beard.

"I'll do the job."

For however long he was here. His stay in San Rey was supposed to have been temporary, but between his father's failing health and his mother's forgetfulness— for lack of a better word—there was more than enough to tie him up in this town longer than he'd intended.

The next thing he knew, he'd been elected sheriff. Elected was stretching it. The mayor had appointed him. His dad had a heavy hand in that. At the time, he didn't want to let his old man down and agreed to step in temporarily until his brother Adam came home or they found someone else for the job. Someone like Pax.

The need to get the hell out of San Rey pulled at him. Not that there was anything left in L.A. He'd pretty much burned through whatever peace he'd found there. He could start over someplace else. San Diego, maybe. The bigger the city, the easier to blend in. Some place where everyone and their mother didn't know *everything* about him. Somewhere it didn't matter whose son he was. Where generations didn't stand on his shoulders, expecting him to be someone he wasn't.

Graham handed his dad a pair of latex gloves. "Here. Put these on if you're going to stick around. And I know you will."

Ham snapped the gloves on. "Like it or not, the town is depending on you. I'm depending on you. There are worse places to live, worse things you could do with your life, you know."

He went into the house, leaving Graham alone on the porch with his resentment and frustration. Guilt was there, too, along with the five-generation deep responsibility his father had instilled in him. He'd do the job, damn it. As long as he was sheriff, he'd do the job.

Graham headed into the house after his father, stopping on the threshold to take in the scene from this view. Deidre lay nearest the door. The old Formica dining set Greg's parents had back when Graham hung around was one of the few pieces of furniture still in the house. A purse sat on the floor near the chair closest to the door. A stack of papers had been placed at the head of the table. He stepped over Deidre's legs, careful to avoid the blood pooled around her body.

She'd been shot in the stomach and the bloody marks on the floor made it look as though she'd tried to crawl toward something—the backdoor or her purse? —before the blood loss had probably made her too weak. So why was she laying face up? Had the killer rolled her over? Or Greg? Or less likely, Erin?

Deidre had been pretty. Greg hadn't mentioned her or their troubles when they'd run into each other last week. But then Graham hadn't given much time to his old friend. He regretted that now. He should've gotten that beer Greg had offered, touched base with him. Graham wondered what they'd been like as a couple. What had happened for them to end up as they were now?

He scanned the document at the top of the stack. Divorce papers. No surprise. Their break up was the talk of the town. San Rey was nothing if not a hot bed of rumor and gossip. Nothing happened in this town that every single citizen didn't know about. That was one of the reasons he'd left, wanting to go someplace where no one knew him, his family, and his screw ups. But the anonymity he'd found in L.A. didn't shield him from making new mistakes.

With gloved fingers, he lifted a couple of papers by

the edge, quickly reading through the settlement nego-tiations. Deidre had signed them. Greg hadn't. Was that why she'd come here, to get his signature? He made note of the name of Deidre's attorney. He'd follow up with him. Greg's family might know something about the couple and the terms of their divorce if the lawyer wouldn't talk.

Graham bent and took a cursory look at the contents of Deidre's purse. There was the usual female junk—a wallet, some lip stuff, keys, a mirror, brush, a couple of receipts, and a prescription bottle of Na-tabs. Whatever that was.

From his crouched level, Graham studied the layout of the room and the position of the bodies. Near the backdoor he noticed some dirt. No, sawdust.

"Got something?" Pax leaned against the doorframe between the kitchen and living room, a little less green than he'd been before.

"Yeah." Graham stood. "Sawdust by the backdoor. Make sure the team sees that. And don't lean against the jam. I want this scene as undisturbed as possible. That includes any DNA or outside material that may be on our clothing. Does anything here strike you as odd?"

Pax straightened away from the door. To his credit, he didn't seem annoyed at being corrected by someone younger with less years on the force than him. Someone who had essentially stepped over him to take the position as sheriff.

"In what way?" Pax asked.

"Why would Greg wait until Erin came in to shoot himself?"

"He'd been busted? Didn't want to go to jail?"

"Maybe." He stepped back over to Pax's side of the room, examining the scene from this new angle. "But Erin said she had to find a key in the pot to let herself in. Greg could have just taken off through the back door, then come in after Erin found the body."

"I see what you're saying," Pax said. He might not have the same crime scene experience as Graham, but Pax was a sharp guy. He would've worked through all this on his own if he'd been the one to talk with Erin. "If he came in after Erin," Pax continued, "he'd throw suspicion off of himself and onto an anonymous someone else. Sweet Jesus. This means we've got our self a real murderer. In San Rey."

"Maybe."

"But you just said—"

"I'm asking questions. Working through the possibilities."

Ham walked up behind Pax and clapped him on the shoulder. "I told you he was good."

"It's a good thing *he's* sheriff," Pax responded. "None of the rest of us has any experience with a scene like this."

Pax didn't catch the way Ham's gaze dropped or the way his lips pressed down at the corners, but Graham did. His father didn't like being lumped in with the rest of them.

"Let's get out of here." Graham motioned for them to move ahead of him. "The less people through here, the better."

They moved into the living room. Curtains pulled

tight over the windows caved the room, making it difficult to navigate now that the sun was almost down. Graham pulled a flashlight off his belt and switched it on.

"I can hit the lights," Pax said.

"No. No one touches anything. The lab guys will bring in their own lights. Pop, why don't you hang out on the porch? I want Pax to go with me to take a look at the other rooms."

"Sure." Ham moved to the front door, his shoulders hunched and hard.

Graham knew his dad felt put out to pasture, but he wasn't a cop anymore. He was supposed to be taking care of himself, not unnecessarily stressing himself. Besides, this wasn't kids stealing candy bars from Lucky's or making sure Billy Dean got home after drinking himself under a bar. This was murder. The scene was complicated and ugly. There was so much more going on here than the small town sheriff deputies were prepared for. He doubted if most of them had even seen a dead body before.

"How about I stop by when I'm finished if it's not too late?" Graham offered Ham in consolation to get him to go home and rest. "Run a few things past you, get your take on things?"

Ham gave a firm nod, his stiffness easing. "Sounds good. Your mother made coffee cake this morning. I'll save you a piece, make us some herb tea." He said the last as though the words were bitter. Losing his coffee had been nearly as difficult as losing his job.

"Only if you spike it."

"Only if you don't tell your mother."

"Tell her what?" Graham watched his father turn up the collar on his trench coat and go out the door with a backwards wave.

"That was a good thing you did," Pax said so only Graham could hear.

Graham shook off the compliment. Having his dad around complicated things. He couldn't be Ham Doran's son *and* sheriff. His men had already shown deference toward their ex-sheriff. He didn't want to have to compete with his father for the deputies' loyalty while working his friend's case.

"Let's take a look at the other rooms." Graham started out with Pax following.

They edged down a short hall to a bedroom. The room Greg had shared with his brother and where Graham had slept on the floor during sleepovers. Graham swept the beam of his flashlight around the room. Old memories competed with the new emptiness of the space. The only furniture in the room was an upright dresser that had seen better days. The drawers stood open, gap toothed and forgotten. They'd been cleaned out, but Graham ran the light over them top and bottom as best he could without disturbing them, remembering how Greg liked to tape things to the bottom to hide them from his brother. Nothing.

They moved on down the hall to the only bathroom. It, too, had been stripped. Its bare bones exposed, the scent of baths and showers long since gone. All that remained was the slight stench of mildew and neglect.

The last room was the largest, the master bedroom. Graham could still remember the smell of Greg's mother's perfume. It hung in the stale air—another ghost of better times. This room stood empty except for a handful of orphaned hangers in the closet.

He had so many memories of better times spent here with Greg. The house was small, but it had sheltered the Lasiters for years. There was nothing left here but the carcass of a home, picked clean of its warmth and spirit.

"I think we're done," Graham said.

"Yeah," Pax replied on a heavy exhale.

They made their way back to the living room. Pax went outside while Graham took a moment to wander around the largest room of the house. He could almost smell the chocolate chip cookies Mrs. Lasiter would have waiting when they came home from school and hear Mr. Lasiter yell for them to be quiet while he watched his show. Memories of time spent here with Greg floated in and out with the reality that the Lasiters would only ever be that now—a memory.

He paced the room, ending up back at the front door, having achieved nothing except a raw ache in his belly. He stopped on his way outside to examine the front door. The key stood out proud from the lock. He hit it with the beam of the flashlight, noting what appeared to be particles of soil stuck to it, confirming what Erin had told him. Stepping out on the porch, he found the pot Erin must have pulled it from. Soil topped the rim and some of it had spilled over onto the deck of the porch.

Erin.

He caught her watching him from the back of his cruiser. She looked pissed. And cold. He cursed himself for leaving her out here all this time, then chuckled under his breath as he imagined all the ways *she'd* probably been cursing him. He checked in with Pax and told him to have the crime scene guys photograph and enter the key in the door as evidence. He rattled off a few more instructions, conscious of Erin's gaze boring into the back of his head.

By the time he started for his car, she was shaking in outrage... or was she shivering? Damn. He should have turned the heater on for her.

He pulled the car door open and got in. "Sorry. Didn't think it would take that long."

"Sur-r-r-re."

He turned the key and cranked the heater up. "No. Really."

"You c-c-could have l-l-least given me a b-b-blanket."

"Ah, no. I couldn't. Evidence transfer and all."

She whispered something under her breath and glared out the window.

"What was that?"

"Ass-s-s-hole."

"How ladylike and dainty you are."

"F-f-fuck off."

"Original and clever, too. You should be feeling the heat now."

Her furious gaze met his in the rearview mirror. "Like you c-c-care."

He stretched his arm across the passenger seat so he could look backwards as he reversed the car. "Actually I do. Some evidence can be destroyed or damaged if it's subjected to frigid temperatures."

She made a frustrated noise and kicked the divider that separated the rows of seats.

He stifled a laugh. "Watch it. I wouldn't want to have to arrest you for destroying city property."

Her flushed cheeks puffed in and out and she shot him the bird with both hands. He shifted his gaze from the rearview mirror to the road, pretending he hadn't seen her gesture, and resisted the urge to make a crack about how he'd like to take her up on her offer. He drove past the crowd of gawkers as quickly as possible, wanting to shield Erin as much as possible. It was probably a wasted effort. The first arrivals would have filled in the newcomers and so on in a twisted game of small town Telephone.

"Give me your aunt's number and I'll call her so she can meet us at the station with a change of clothes for you."

"She already knows-s-s."

"You didn't call her, did you? I should have confiscated your cell phone. I didn't want you talking to anyone before giving your statement."

"I don't have to call her for her to know."

Graham shifted in his seat and adjusted his grip on the steering wheel. He'd never believed the rumors about Cerie December being some kind of clairvoyant. Talk like that in a small town was usually that—just talk. People said all kinds of shit to further their own agendas or to be plain old mean. He should know. The town's opinion of him wasn't anywhere near accurate. He wasn't now nor would he ever be the golden boy returned.

"Give me her number." He punched it in his cell phone as she rattled it off.

"Hello, Sheriff." Erin's Aunt Cerie answered before the first ring. "How's your father?"

"Well, thank you. I'm calling because Erin needs you to—"

"Bring her a change of clothes. Yes, I know. I'm at the station. Waiting."

"Yes, ma'am."

"Tell her that I've brought her a Thermos of tea as well. She's so cold *I'm* shivering."

"Yes, ma'am."

"And Graham?"

"Yes?"

"*I* have faith in you." Cerie hung up before Graham could respond. *What the hell did that mean?*

"Told you," Erin said, her voice stronger.

Graham thumbed the End button on his phone, unsettled by his conversation with Cerie. Not because of the supposed psychic thing... oh, hell, who was he kidding? The woman was sweet, but that conversation creeped the shit out of him.

It was the *way* she'd said her parting remark that threw him. *She* had faith in him. Did that mean others didn't? Had she picked up on something he hadn't? He couldn't ask her without giving away his own doubts.

Had he missed something at the scene? Should he have stayed until the investigators arrived?

No. He refused to believe that. It was being back in this damned town. He'd never second-guessed himself in L.A. Well, almost never. He'd never let a crazy supposed psychic like Cerie December get to him, that's for sure. He'd run cases on his own before. Had closed a good portion of them, a better than average portion of them.

He knew what he was doing, damn it.

"Mabel would have told her what happened," Erin said, breaking into his thoughts. "That I was involved. Plus Aunt Cerie took my car this morning because hers is on the fritz so she knew I would've walked to Greg's house from the office. And then the rain came faster and harder than the weather announcer had said it would. Hence the dry clothes."

"Are you telling me your aunt's not really psychic? If that's the case, she shouldn't be taking money from people for her 'readings.' That's fraud."

"She's smart *and* psychic. Not to mention best friends with your dispatcher who uses her head set as a megaphone."

"Can't defend that."

"You can turn the heat down. I'm warmer now and you're probably burning up."

He was sweating his balls off. "I'm okay."

The uncomfortable silence grew into a solid mass between them. If they weren't exchanging barbs, he hardly knew how to talk to her. He stole looks at her in the rear view mirror, flicking his gaze over the parts of her he could see. He didn't want to get caught staring.

She faced away, her attention on the scenery out the window. Her hair was beginning to dry and curled in clumps around her face. She must have been standing fairly close to Greg when he'd shot himself. Bits of gore had gotten caught in her hair. He frowned over that.

Still, she was beautiful. There was a fragility to her that belied her fiery personality. She looked made of china, the kind his Grandma Byrne only put out on special occasions because it was fine and old, having passed through several generations. And like the danger of handling his grandma's china, he had to suppress the urge to touch her, run the tips of his fingers along her jaw, her collarbone to make sure she was real. Something as delicate as she belonged to the faery stories Grandma Byrne had told him as a boy.

They pulled up to the police station, which was a Victorian house that had been converted sometime in the seventies. They'd ripped all the gingerbread off the façade, leaving it with awkwardly angled roofs and a tower that looked more like a missile silo than a graceful turret.

Graham grabbed the umbrella from his trunk and came around to let Erin out. He held the umbrella over her head as they climbed the steps.

At the top she turned to him, holding her arms out. "Will I be able to shower before I change into clean clothes?"

"There's a shower in the bathroom at the back."

"Thank God."

Graham opened the door for her and followed her inside. They hit the wall of women two steps in.

"Is it really mur—"

"What hap—"

"I was so wor—"

Jessica, Mabel and Cerie got a look at Erin and froze, eyes wide, mouths gaping.

"Let me get Erin back to the bathroom so she can shower and change." Graham held his hand out. "Cerie, her clothes?"

"What? Oh." Cerie handed him a bag. "Erin, dear, are you all right? Please tell me none of that blood is yours."

"I'm fine. None of it's mine."

Jessica wrinkled her nose like she smelled something bad.

"You poor thing," Mabel chimed in. "You look like a drowned gutter rat."

"Why don't I help you change?" Cerie said, reaching for Erin's arm.

"No. No one touch her." He gestured for Erin to precede him.

The women jumped back, their eyes wider than before. Erin walked ahead of him down the hall to his office. Once inside, he closed the door after them.

"I'm sorry about that," he said, noticing how pale she was.

She shrugged. "It's all right."

"I need to take a couple of pictures of you. You know, to document the evidence." He was sweating from more than the hot car ride. Why was he suddenly so nervous?

"Where should I stand?"

"Right there's fine." He went to his desk and pulled out a camera.

"Is it okay if I don't smile?"

He looked up from the viewfinder at her remark. "You don't have to." He snapped a couple of pictures, then set the camera aside to rummage around in his desk drawer. "Are you right or left handed?"

"Right. Why?"

"Hold out your hands palms down. I need to test for gunshot residue although it's likely the rain washed it away."

"*What?*"

"*If* there is any, I mean. I know there won't be. It's just procedure. Sorry."

She pressed her lips together, making a muscle at her jaw twitch as she stuck her hands out for his inspection. He pretended not to notice them shaking as he pulled on a pair of latex gloves and slowly approached her. He swabbed both sides of her right, then the left hand, paying particular attention to the web area between her thumbs and index fingers.

"All done," he said. "I'll get the evidence bags now."

"Evidence bags?"

"For your clothes and what I'm going to pull from your hair." When her hand automatically went to her hair he stopped her. "Don't. Cross contamination."

"Oh, right." She stood still, her hands out to her sides.

He changed gloves and moved toward her again with caution. She looked as though she'd shatter under the slightest touch. He wanted to tell her it would be okay and somehow soften the things she'd witnessed. He couldn't say that he knew her or how she'd react if he tried. Mostly he knew things about her, which was worse than not knowing anything at all because he had no way to sort the truth from the fiction. He cursed small town life and the traps it laid.

Pulling bits of matter from her hair with tweezers, he was careful not to accidentally catch a strand or let her see what he put in the collection bag. There was something strangely intimate between them in that moment. He hoped he wasn't imagining it at the same time he mentally kicked himself for thinking it. He'd never been this close to her before, had never inhaled her scent or touched her in anyway. Now here they were, sharing personal space and trying not to make eye contact.

When he finished he took a step back, exhaling the breath he'd been holding. "Done." He pointed to a door across the room. "That's the bathroom. There should be a towel and washcloth in the cabinet under the sink."

"Thanks."

"Leave the door ajar."

She paused and turned to look at him, a questioning frown buckling her brows.

"Chain of evidence," he replied, holding out a pair of gloves for her. "Put these on before you ah... undress."

Taking the gloves, she nodded and continued on her way. She left the door partially open, as he'd asked. This was the first time he'd spent any time with her. All the years he'd known her—or more accurately, known *of* her—there had always been people around. They'd never been in a room together—alone. He'd never truly noticed her. He was noticing her now and that new awareness did strange things to his ability to keep things strictly business.

He changed gloves, grabbed a few more evidence bags and approached the door. "Hand me your coat first."

"Am I going to get any of these clothes back?"

"Do you want them back?"

She opened the door and handed him her coat and shoes. "No, I suppose not."

He took them from her one at a time and bagged them. "Are you sure you're okay? You look a little pale."

"I j-just saw myself in the mirror."

"Damn. I'm sorry. I should've covered it or something."

She pulled the door so she was hidden again. "Too late."

He heard the movement of fabric and then she poked her hand out of the gap in the doorway, offering her blouse. He put it in a bag, trying not to imagine what color her bra would be. Then her bra was thrust through the opening. Purple. And warm from her body. Did her panties match?

Next came her skirt and he found himself getting twitchy, his clothes chafing. Her hand appeared with a wadded up ball of fabric. He couldn't bring himself to take them from her and nudged her arm with the opening of the bag. She dropped them inside. Light blue cotton. He was so fixated, trying to imagine them on her that it took him a moment to realize she was standing on the other side of the door completely naked.

3

Graham sat at his desk, trying to suppress the images his brain kept tossing up of Erin in the shower. He updated his notes from the crime scene. *Erin's head tipped back, her fingers sliding through her hair, water skimming her bare skin.* He checked in with Pax. *Erin bent over, her soapy hands gliding down her legs.* He flipped the radio on to drown out the sound of the shower. *Erin soaping her breasts, her hand slipping lower—*

A knock on his door brought his head up. Cerie stood in the doorway, leaning against the frame, arms crossed. She wore some kind of flowing dress with long sleeves that hung like wings from her arms. He should've heard her coming with all the bells and charms hanging from her neck and wrists. She'd tied her graying dark hair into a long braid that hung over one shoulder. Graham saw Erin in the softened lines and creases of Cerie's face. If she were anything like her aunt, Erin would age well, growing gracefully into her later years.

"Your thoughts are so vivid I feel the need to check myself for an erection."

"Excuse me?"

She strolled in and looked around. No doubt wondering where Erin was. Graham had always thought of her as eccentric, but harmless. Or was that just semantics for insane?

"I prefer eccentric over insane."

"I never said—"

"And no, Erin can't read thoughts like I do. Her talents lie elsewhere." Cerie smoothed her skirt and sat without being invited. "It's a good thing for you since you broadcast yours like an air raid siren. Thank you for the compliment by the way. We've been blessed with Great Grandma December's genes."

He sat back in his chair. If not crazy then...what? He'd heard the rumors about the Decembers. Cerie seemed to be the only one who traded on them, offering her services as a medium in exchange for money. Donald, Erin's father, kept mostly to himself, but there was talk about him too that naturally spilled over onto Erin. Were they psychics or just...odd?

"Why bother having conversations with people when you can pluck the thoughts straight from their heads?" he asked.

"Because that would be terribly one sided and I enjoy talking so very much."

His lips twitched. He'd always liked Cerie, despite

the whispers of her being a witch. "Is there something I can help you with?"

"Actually there is. Something's happened."

He made a motion for her to continue. He couldn't wait to see what she'd come up with. Ghosts maybe, or ghouls.

"Besides the murder/suicide. The poor dears." She closed her eyes as though she were praying.

"Cerie? Your point?"

She opened her eyes and sat up straighter. "I think it's the storm. It seems to be affecting our abilities."

"*Our* abilities?"

"I suspect it might have something to do with the storm on top of the full moon and mercury being in retrograde."

"You don't seem to be having any...issues."

"Not at the moment, no. But earlier I was doing a reading for Bessie Farnsworth's daughter Beatrice. You'd remember her. She's about your age. Blond. She's expecting... Beatrice, not Bessie you understand—"

"Of course."

"Anywho, there I was, the Tarot deck all laid out, then... blink!"

"Blink."

"Blink! Nothin'. Nada. Zilch. My mind went as blank as Bessie's head."

"Is this leading somewhere because I have a lot of work to do here, Cerie?"

"I'll let you get back to your X-rated imaginings of my niece in a moment."

He let the grin go, liking how it stretched little-used muscles. "That would be nice."

"At the first clap of thunder... blink, blank, bloop." She passed a dramatic hand across her face. "Nothing." She lowered her hand and leaned forward. "Reading Bessie's always been like reading a news flicker, which is why she's one of my best customers, you understand. So you can imagine my concern when she went blank as the side of a barn."

"I'm still not seeing as how this is police business."

"It's not. It's Erin business. And if you're meaning to make Erin your business you better work on that properly or stop putting her in the starring role of your own private porno. Got me?"

He had no business making Erin his business. Fantasizing about her was one thing, acting on it was another. "Get around to it or get out of my office so I can do my work."

"Donald said the same thing's been happening to him off and on all day."

"Donald."

"You remember, Erin's father. Boy, it's a good thing I'm the only mind reader in the family or you'd be staring down the double barrel of Grandpa December's shotgun. I'm telling you. That shotgun's not the only thing Donald inherited from Grandpa D." She put her hand to the side of her mouth. "Both he and Erin got Grandpa's terrible temper."

"How does this relate to Erin?"

"If my ability went on the fritz and Donald's too, then Erin's must have as well."

He jerked upright. "Erin has an ability?" Why didn't he know this about her?

"She doesn't like anyone to know so this will have to fall under client confidentiality."

"I'm a cop, not a lawyer."

She waved that away. "Whatever. The point is, I'm worried for Erin and I need you to help me keep an eye on her. Since you seem to like eyeing her, I figured you're the perfect one for the job. Plus, I trust you."

"Thank you. I think. Just what kind of secret ability does Erin have?"

A commotion out in the front office caught their attention.

"White bread and fruit punch," Cerie mumbled.

"What?"

"Here he comes. The most staid man in the county, maybe the state. He won't be much competition for you." She winked. "But Donald likes him so that could be a potential problem."

"I would ask what you're talking about, but I have a feeling I'm better off not knowing."

"Erin has visions," Cerie hurriedly whispered. "Of the past and future." She pressed a finger to her lips. "Remember. Mum's the word."

He opened his mouth to ask her more, but Keith Collins appeared in the doorway.

"Oh. Hello. I didn't know you'd be here," he said to Graham.

"It's my office."

"I'm looking for Erin—"

The bathroom door opened and Erin walked out,

towel drying her hair. "Keith." She stumbled to a stop. "What are you doing here?"

Cerie repositioned her chair to take in the scene. "This ought to be good."

Graham stood up and came around his desk. He had an overwhelming urge to drag Erin out of the room and ask her what the hell her aunt had been talking about. Erin had the ability to see the past and future? How?

"So it's true," Keith said, crumpling a little in his starched white shirt.

"What's true?" Erin asked.

"You've been arrested," Keith answered.

Graham folded his arms. This whole business was getting ridiculous. "Who says she's been arrested?"

"It's all over town," Keith said. "Carol in produce told me that Janet from the pharmacy's son told *her* that he saw you being taken to jail in the back of the sheriff's car. So I came right down to bail you out." He fidgeted a little in his Lucky's Bag N Save apron, his employee of the month pins winking under the florescent lighting.

This was why he couldn't wait to get out of San Ray. He studied Erin. And wondered why if she had this supposed ability, she'd kept it a secret all these years. "Goddamned small town." And then he realized he'd answered his own question right there.

Erin inwardly sighed. Keith really was a nice guy. She wished all over again that she could like him more.

Guys who would overlook her aunt's quirkiness *and* offer to bail her out of jail weren't thick on the ground.

"Humph. I knew it!" Aunt Cerie said, glancing between Keith and Erin.

Damn it. She'd lowered her defenses and her aunt had read her thoughts about Keith. She shored them back up and turned to Keith. "I'm not under arrest. I'm a witness."

Cerie drew up in her chair and folded her arms, glaring at Erin. "I hate that you can block me out."

"A witness?" Keith crossed the room in two long-legged strides. He put his hands on either side of her face. The gesture was meant to be endearing, but was ruined by the coldness of his hands and how they always smelled like the bottom of a freezer. "My poor angel face."

Behind Keith, Aunt Cerie put her hands to her throat and stuck her tongue out like she was choking.

Keith's brows drew together and his lips pressed flat. He was worried about her. In his eyes Erin saw how much he cared and she wished all over again that she could return his feelings. There was absolutely nothing wrong with him. He was a handsome hometown boy, clean and well dressed, his hair always combed. He had fresh breath and a good job with benefits. To top it off, last year he'd bought a house that he was fixing up, perfect for a family. Keith belonged to the community in a way Erin never had. On paper he was everything she should have wanted.

But with Keith, she always felt one step behind with no hope of ever catching up. She should've broken things off long before now. Whenever she summoned the courage to try, he'd say or do something sweet and she'd think that maybe if she gave it more time, she'd develop feelings for him. He was nearly perfect in every way. She was beginning to think there must be something wrong with *her*.

"I'm all right," she told Keith, accepting his kiss.

Aunt Cerie jumped up, putting her hands to her head. "Ouch! Rats and skeletons, it's happening again."

Keith broke away from Erin to stare at her aunt like he thought she could actually produce rats and skeletons.

"What's happening?" Graham asked.

"Blink, blank, bloop."

"Is she... well?" Keith whispered in Erin's ear.

Erin pretended she didn't hear him. She'd gotten good at pretending with Keith. "What's wrong, Auntie?"

"Something else is going on here," Aunt Cerie said to Graham. "It's not the storm." She rubbed her temples.

Erin didn't like how pale her aunt was or how shaky her hands were. Cerie never got sick. "Are you okay?"

Graham moved closer to Cerie. "What makes you say that?"

Aunt Cerie started for the door. "I need to talk to Donald."

"Auntie, wait."

Erin moved to follow her aunt, but Graham caught her elbow. "You stay."

She tried to wiggle free. "I have to find out what's wrong with her."

"It's nothing you can help her with right now and I can't let you leave before getting your formal statement."

She rounded on him, but it was Keith who stepped between them, breaking Graham's hold.

Keith put his arm around her shoulders. "Not a word until your lawyer gets here."

"My lawyer?"

"That's a smart move," Graham said. "You should have representation."

"But I'm just a witness."

"We'll be testing the samples I took from your hands and hair, and sending your clothes to the lab as evidence. They'll be testing for DNA and gunshot residue among other things."

"What *other things*?" Keith asked.

"Signs that Erin might have had a personal relationship with either Greg Lasiter or his wife."

Graham said it so casually as though it was a normal thing for him to accuse someone of murdering her lover. Worse yet, accusing *Erin* of murdering her *married* lover. Is that what he thought of her? Is that what the whole town would think happened?

"*What?*" Keith went as white as his shirt.

"You think I was sleeping with Greg Lasiter?" She could hardly see Graham for the red haze that filled her vision.

"Or his wife," Graham added. Was he trying to bait her or Keith?

"His wife," Keith repeated, teetering a little on his feet.

"Actually, no. I don't think you had a personal relationship with either one of them," Graham said. "But I do have to run every possibility. And a witness having a personal relationship with one or more of the victims is a possibility. I'm sorry," he added with a shrug. "It's what I have to do."

She barely managed to control the emotions tripping over themselves inside her. Anger warred with shock, which wrestled disappointment that fought with hurt, all of them brewing a storm to beat the one raging outside. "So basically what you're saying is that you're treating me like a suspect." Her voice cracked, trying to get past the knot in her throat.

"A suspect? I don't believe it. Erin wouldn't hurt a spider." Keith's voice was strong with conviction, but his gaze shifted away.

"Everyone's a suspect until they're ruled out." Graham poked a finger at Keith's name badge. "Even the manager of Lucky's Bag N Save. You knew the Lasiters. They probably shopped in your store. Can you account for your whereabouts today?"

"My whereabouts? Today?" Keith squeaked.

"Hang on. Let me grab my notebook."

"Graham, stop it. You know he didn't have anything to do with this." She turned to Keith. "He's pulling your leg."

Keith adjusted his apron. "I knew that."

"Hello?" Elmer Farnsworth III, Esquire, shuffled into the room. "I'm here about my client, Ellen December."

"It's *Erin*, Mr. Farnsworth," Keith said, ushering the

elderly lawyer into the room. "Thank you for coming on such short notice."

Graham pointed at Elmer. "*He's* her lawyer? Is his license still valid?"

Elmer shook his cane at Graham. "Since before your daddy was a twinkle in his daddy's eye."

Erin pressed her hands to her face. "Tell me this isn't happening."

"He's the best lawyer in town," Keith said.

Graham muttered, "God help us."

"He's the *only* lawyer in town," Erin said, dropping her hands.

Elmer pointed his cane at Erin. "Not true. My granddaughter just passed her bar exam." He rocked back on his heels. "A proud moment indeed."

"Brilliant," Graham said. "And where is *she*?"

"She's... ah... celebrating. Just received the good news today." Elmer checked his pocket watch. "Can we get on with the business at hand? Bingo at Saint Paul's starts at eight and I don't want to get stuck sitting beside Alvin Buttertin again. He farts like a rabid dog and blames it on the person next to him." He nudged Keith's arm. "Can't have the ladies thinking I'll stink up the boudoir, am I right, son?"

"Er... sure."

Graham jabbed a thumb at Elmer. "Are you sure you want him for your lawyer?"

She sighed. "Why not?" How could things get any worse?

"Then have a seat by my desk and we'll get on with it. I'll have to ask you to leave, Keith. Police business.

Sorry." Graham didn't sound sorry as he showed Keith the door.

"I'll wait to drive you home, Erin," Keith said as he left. "I'll just be out front."

"Uh-huh. You do that." Graham shut the door and came around to sit behind his desk. "Do you mind if I record our conversation, Erin?"

"No." She struggled to catch up. Everything was happening all at once. "I guess not."

He pulled a recorder out of his desk drawer and started it. He rattled off the time, date, place, and other salient information. "Okay, Erin. Start from the beginning. Tell me why you went to the Lasiters.'"

"My boss gave me the file on the Lasiter house."

"Where do you work? What's your boss's name?"

"Oh, right. Earlier today my boss, Ramie Singh of Kavender Investments, gave me the file on 321 Amiable Lane, also known as the Lasiter house. My job was to meet with Greg Lasiter to exchange the keys to his house for a check for fifteen hundred dollars. This saved the company time and money from having to forcibly remove Greg...er, Mr. Lasiter, from the house and change the locks. We had an appointment to meet today at four o'clock at Mr. Lasiter's house."

Should she mention the vision she had when she'd received the file and then again after she spoke to Greg? The visions had been wrong... no, incomplete. Greg had fallen in almost the same position in her vision as he had in reality. She closed her eyes, bringing up her vision and picturing it side by side with what she remembered. It was like putting two photos next to each other and comparing them. His body position was the same. The gun in his hand the same. But Deidre wasn't in her vision. The table and chairs weren't either. Why were they so different?

"Erin? Are you all right?"

She touched a hand to her forehead and opened her eyes. "No. I mean, yes. I'm fine."

"You had an appointment with Mr. Lasiter," Graham prompted. "Then what?"

"I had to walk to his house because my aunt had my car. It wasn't far, only a few blocks."

A blinding flash of light. A jolt. She was suddenly back on Amiable Lane. The wind tangled her hair and slipped into her coat. She shivered. The sky was black, the clouds almost close enough to touch. She could smell the ocean and the sweet scent of impending rain. Her mind skipped like a scratched record and then she was at the back of the house, on the porch. She'd never been at the back of the house, but she somehow knew that's where she was. She reached a hand out to knock on the door except her arm was longer, her hand larger. She wasn't herself. She was a man.

This was new. She'd never taken over a body in her visions. Trapped. There was no other word for it. She was trapped in this body *and* this vision. Would she be able to get out of it? Somewhere in another time she shivered.

The man's other hand—her hand, his hand—held a gun snug in the pocket of his coat. He gripped the gun harder, the squeak of his leather gloves almost deafening in the silence. Annoyance. Anger. Shame. He had to stop Deidre. Should've gotten rid of her sooner. This had gone too far. Deidre had taken things too seriously. But oh, how he wished he could screw Deidre just once more. He loved the way Deidre's breasts bounced when she was on top, riding him. The way Deidre made him feel when he was with her, inside her. He was a king with Deidre.

He knocked on the door, plastered on a smile. Deidre answered. He'd always remember Deidre in this moment, the way she smiled up at him, happy, worshipful. Like he was a freaking hero. But then Deidre had to go and ruin it all by getting pregnant. He pulled the gun from his pocket—

Blinding light shattered the vision. Pain split Erin's head. She fell forward, vaguely aware of Graham saying something, holding her. And then, just as suddenly as it had come, the light and pain were gone.

"Erin. Can you hear me?"

She blinked up at Graham, the light fixture overhead haloing him. *What's happening?*

Opening her eyes fully, she realized she was in his lap on the floor. He smoothed her hair back from her face. His hands were warm and gentle, not cold. They smelled like soap.

"What happened?" he asked.

"I..." *What?* What could she tell him? Someone or something was interfering with her ability, getting into her head and bending her visions. There was almost a purposefulness to it, as though a tripwire had been installed in her brain, triggering a trap.

"This young lady isn't well enough to give her statement," Elmer said, slipping his watch back in his pocket. He stood up. "I'm calling a halt to these interrogations until the young miss is well enough to sustain them." He thumped his cane on the floor to punctuate his point and left for his bingo game.

Graham's eyes had a curious blue-black ring around the paler blue of his irises. His lashes looked like they'd been tipped with gold. He stared down at her with concern and something that felt strangely like interest. He lifted a strand of hair off her face. "Tell me what's wrong."

It *was* interest. She blinked up at him, caught by an unexpected answering tug of longing. His gaze dropped to her mouth and for a moment she thought he might kiss her. She *wanted* him to kiss her. This had to stop. She had a boyfriend. What was she doing entertaining these thoughts, let alone encouraging them? She pushed at him, trying to scramble off his lap.

In her haste she accidentally planted her palm on his groin.

He doubled over, knocking his head against hers.

They both jerked back. "Ow!" they said in unison, then, "Sorry."

Graham had one hand on his crotch and one on his head and suddenly it was all too much for her. This whole thing was ridiculous. The very idea of them was ridiculous. She burst into giggles. Graham's concern morphed into surprise, and then laughter. His laugh was deep and rich, the sexy throatiness of it arrowed straight through her. She reached out to touch the bump on his forehead, lifting strands of hair away with the tips of her fingers. He caught her wrist and their laughter slowed, then died altogether. Frozen in the moment, she couldn't look away. He held her gaze, then slowly turned his head and kissed the underside of her wrist. She lost her breath.

Mirroring her, he reached out and touched his fingertips to her forehead, then trailed them around her face to her temple, her cheek, her jaw. His gaze followed the movement as though memorizing the curve of her face.

"So soft," he whispered.

She clasped his wrist, stilling his hand.

"Tell me what happened," he said, pulling her ever so slightly toward him.

She couldn't look away, didn't want to pull away, caught by whatever was going on between them. "I-I'm not sure."

"No?"

"No."

"Erin, I know."

She shook her head. He couldn't.

"I know about you. I know *all* about you."

All about her? The hard thump of her heart echoed in her ears. He was close, so close. She felt herself arching toward him as though he were a magnet. Everything else in the room faded and it was just him and her and this overwhelming link they seemed to share.

"You can't."

"I do." His breath whispered across her skin as he

leaned closer. "I know about your ability. I know some-thing's wrong, something's happening to you."

She thought to deny it, then nodded. Unable to resist.

"Tell me about it. Let me help you."

4

The loud thump of a door closing broke through the haze that had invaded Erin's brain. She shook her head, suddenly realizing where she was and whom she was with.

What the hell just happened?

She'd almost told Graham her secret, that's what. No good could come from that. He'd never understand. How could she explain the unexplainable? What if he told other people about her? What if he told Keith?

Then another thought struck. *How did he know about her ability?*

"You can't help me." She pulled free and stood. Too many things were happening inside her. She couldn't catalog them all fast enough to put them neatly in their slots to deal with later. She had to get out of there.

He rose and shook his head as though he didn't understand what had just happened either. "What was that?"

She didn't think he was only talking about her

collapse. Hugging herself to ward off the sudden chill, she shook her head. She had no answers for him.

Graham watched her closely. "You know what I think—"

"Elmer left," Keith said from the doorway.

Erin started. She'd been so focused on trying to figure out what Graham did and didn't know about her that she hadn't noticed Keith's entrance.

"He said you were sick or something." Keith walked over and put his arm around her. "Are you feeling okay, angel face?"

"Not really."

"You're pale and you've been through so much. Let me take you home." Keith gave Graham a look that dared him to argue.

"I can finish getting your statement tomorrow." Graham didn't look happy about having to wait. Or was it Keith's sudden appearance? Had something gone on between them that she didn't know about?

Erin started to gather her things, and realized her cell phone wasn't among them. "My phone's missing." She looked to Graham, thinking maybe he might have taken it.

"I don't have it."

"I must've dropped it at Greg's house."

"We'll look for it tomorrow," Keith said.

"I need it now. I have to call my boss to tell him what happened, plus I need to check in with my aunt and dad."

Keith steered her toward the door. "All right. We'll get it tonight if that's okay with the sheriff."

"One thing," Graham said, causing them to pause in their tracks. "Erin rides with me."

"I don't see why—" Keith began.

"I have to control the scene," Graham interrupted. "I want a tight case. Not that she would, but I don't want anyone to come back and accuse her of tampering with evidence."

"Fine," Keith bit out. "I'll follow you over, then take her home afterward."

"Fine," Graham agreed.

Erin had to endure Jessica's blatant gawking and Mabel's not so stealth staring as they passed through the front office. No doubt tonight's events would be all over town by morning. If they weren't already. Just what she needed—another reason to stand out. She was grateful to finally be out on the porch and out from under their watchful stares.

It was still raining in great sheets, the sound constant and unrelenting. Lightning flashed, followed closely by a loud crack of thunder. The storm hovered over the town like a punishment.

"After this we'll get you home, snuggle up on the couch, and maybe watch a movie or something," Keith said. "How does that sound?"

"Good." It actually kind of did. She didn't want to be alone tonight.

Keith kissed her cheek and went down the steps to his car.

Graham grabbed his umbrella from the stand by the door and opened it. "Let's get you in the car so you can hurry up and do that snuggle movie thing."

Was that sarcasm in Graham's tone?

He took her elbow and helped her into his car. She tried to get a read on him, but the cloud-covered moon darkened the night, making it difficult to see his expression. He tossed the umbrella in the back, climbed in, and started the engine with a hard yank of the key. Something was definitely going on here. More than the deaths of Greg and Deidre, and his supposed knowledge about her ability. She didn't know Graham well enough to know what that something was, but she had a feeling that not all of this controlling the scene business was completely on the up and up.

"That stuff about keeping your eye on me was all bullshit, wasn't it?" she asked.

He hesitated. "Yes and no. I don't want any mistakes on this case and I wanted to talk to you alone without tall, dark and grocerly hanging around." He put the car in reverse and backed out.

More sarcasm directed at her boyfriend.

"What do you have against Keith? He's a good guy."

Frowning, he put the car in drive. "I know."

He hit the gas and their car went ahead of Keith's. She pretended to focus on the passing scenery, but the storm made that impossible.

"Did you *see* something back there?" he asked after a moment.

"I'm not sure what you mean."

"I think you do. Come off it. Tell me what you saw." She didn't answer right away, so he prodded her again. "Erin. I told you, I *know*. You don't have to hide who you are from me."

"That would put you in the minority."

"Along with Keith?"

"No."

After a beat he said, "Did you see something about the Lasiters?"

How could he possibly know about her ability? He'd been hinting about knowing her lifetime-long kept secret since she came to on the floor of his office. She bit the inside of her cheek.

"Cerie's worried about you. She thinks you might be having problems with your your ability, too."

Her *aunt* told him about her ability? Why? Why would she—?

That's why Cerie had rushed out of Graham's office. She must have wanted to get out of there before she had a collapse like Erin's. What did it mean? Had her father been affected, too?

"You can see the past and future." Not a question. There was no judgment or censure in his tone. He wasn't mocking her. Did that mean he believed in psychic abilities?

She'd learned at an early age that the novelty factor of her ability quickly wore off once the reality of what she could do set in. No one liked having the element of surprise taken away from them. No one wanted their past examined. And no one wanted to know how and when a loved one would die. She'd learned that last lesson the hard way.

What would happen if she told Graham about her visions? What would he do with the information? The truth was, she wanted someone besides her family to trust. She was tired of hiding, tired of pretending. She was worn thin from the pretending.

So when he gently said *tell me* again, she fell head-first into the illusion of intimacy in his darkened car. It was just the two of them, not looking at each other with miles of pitch-black road ahead of them.

Starting out unsteadily, then gradually finding her pace, she told him about her initial vision and how it had differed from what had happened at the house.

"Has that ever happened before?" His question was matter of fact, as though he dealt with people with psychic abilities every day.

"Why aren't you freaked out by what I just told you?"

"Who says I'm not?"

She shouldn't have told him. This was a mistake.

"But that doesn't mean I don't believe you," he added. "Or that I'll betray your trust."

"Why?"

"That's not who I am."

Tension she didn't realize she'd been holding drained out of her. That's not who he was. He certainly hadn't reacted the way her mother had when Erin's ability had first started to manifest. Not yet anyway.

"No," she answered his previous question. "My visions have never wavered like that before."

"So it only started when you first touched the file on the Lasiter property."

"Yes."

"Cerie seems to think the storm and the moon and

mercury being in retrograde is messing with *her* ability."

"You're making fun of her."

"I didn't mean it that way. She's...different, that's all I meant. She isn't shy about who she is or using her ability. She trades off of it."

"*Different*. Right."

"You say that like it's a bad thing."

"Do you know what it's like to grow up in my family? Those crazy Decembers. They're witches, they're fakes, they think they're special when all they really want is attention. But mostly, people just think we're nuts."

"Cerie doesn't help your case, I'll give you that."

"When I was a kid I hated that she made her living off giving fortunes."

"And now?"

"It doesn't matter." But it did. More than she wanted to admit. She still hated it, but it was a part of who Cerie was and what she was to the community.

She felt him watching her as they sat at a stoplight, sure he wouldn't let her get away with that answer. She'd confided more in Graham than anyone else, including her family. She'd never told Cerie how she felt about her fortune-telling or any of the rest of it. There was something about Graham that made her want to tell him things. Or maybe it was the exhaustion. Her secret was a heavy and tiresome burden to carry for so long.

"What else did you see about what happened at the Lasiter house?"

Grateful for the subject change, she grabbed at the reprieve he gave her. "In the kitchen with Greg before he... died, I saw Deidre answer the door to her killer."

He gave her a startled glance. "Male or female?"

"Definitely male."

"How can you be sure?"

"He liked it when Deidre was on top when they had sex so he could watch her boobs bounce up and down."

"Who doesn't?"

She glared at him, her mouth dropping open in disgust.

"What?" he teased. "It's true. Ask any guy."

Fighting an answering smile, she rolled her eyes at him. The much-needed moment of levity lingered briefly before Graham had to turn back to the road.

"So Deidre was having an affair with the man who killed her," he said. "Anything else?"

"Deidre's killer shot her because she got pregnant. He was annoyed with her for that."

"Damn. Did you see who he was? Anything about him that you can identify?"

"No, he wore gloves and a dark coat."

"Can you think of anything else?"

"He really got off on being with her. Deidre was in love with him, but she was nothing more than an ego boost for him. While she was divorcing Greg to be with him, hoping he'd divorce his wife, too—he was plotting to get rid of her to protect his marriage and social standing. I didn't like him. At all. It's more than almost being in his skin in my vision when he killed Deidre. He's...sick. His mind isn't right."

"So we're looking for a married man who wanted to stay married. There aren't very many of those." When Erin let the silence stretch, he said, "Sorry. Can't help it."

"Are you mocking me?"

"No—"

"You haven't changed since high school. You're still the same jerk who made fun of my family and me with your friends."

"I never—"

"Yes you did. I heard you. I'm such an idiot for telling you all that, for trusting you." She nearly gagged on her stupidity. This was why she had kept her secret so long, this attitude toward anyone in this town who was different.

"Erin, I swear I never made fun of you."

"I *heard* you, Graham. You and Greg and Mike Deitz and Chris Worley in the library. Mike found a book on circus people."

"I don't remember."

"Of course you don't. But I do. You thought one of the freaks in the book looked like my aunt. That set the rest of them off." Thinking about it now brought back the humiliation as though it was happening all over again. She fought against it. She wasn't that girl anymore. Or at least she was trying really hard not to be.

"I honestly don't remember. We were probably just acting like a bunch of assholes."

"Somebody tore that picture out of the book and glued it to my locker." She wasn't letting him off the hook. Was he really that blithe to what he and his friends had done to her? Was it just a harmless, victim-less prank to them?

"You don't think—"

"On the outside. Where everyone saw it. *Everyone.* They wrote 'Come to the December Freak Show' on it. The custodian had to take the door off my locker and replace it with a new one that was a different color from the rest."

"Jesus."

"That was in February. I had that locker until the end of the year. It made me a target. People shoved nasty notes through the slots almost daily." She pulled in a shaky breath. "Thanks to you and your friends, I was free game."

"Erin, I'm sorry. I don't know which one of my asshole friends did that to you. I'd kick the shit out of him right now if I could."

"You can't." She rubbed her forehead, trying to dislodge the ache that had settled behind her eyes. She sighed. Her anger drained away in the face of their current reality. "It was Greg."

He stopped the car in front of Greg's house and stared at it for a moment. She wished she could read his thoughts. Was he really sorry or only saying it because he'd been forced to face his past actions? How did the new Graham compare to the old? Could she trust him as much as she wanted to? As much as she already had? Or had she made a huge, irreversible mistake here?

Putting his arm across the back of the bench seat,

he turned to her. The look in his eyes was full of regret. And shame. The shame surprised her.

"I really am sorry. I had no idea. I swear. I hope you can forgive me." He glanced at the house again, then back at her. "And Greg."

"I don't know. I'm going to have to wait and see what you do with what I just told you."

"Fair enough, but can I make a suggestion? Please don't repeat what you just said. Someone might think you'd gotten your revenge by killing Greg."

"But I didn't."

He put his hand on her shoulder and squeezed. "I know. *I* know, but someone else might take it differently."

"You know you're a prince when you're not acting like a cop or a smart ass. Unfortunately, that's almost never." She reached for the door handle. "Let's get this over with so I can get away from you." She opened the door and stepped out into the rain, slamming the door behind her.

GRAHAM WOULD'VE KICKED his own ass if it were possible. Why was he pushing her buttons? Just when he'd finally made some progress with her, he ruined it by being a complete fucking idiot. He honestly didn't remember that incident from high school. Was he really that much of an ass back then?

He remembered her very well in high school. She was the only girl who wouldn't give him the time of day. That made her much more interesting than the ones who threw themselves at him. The more he tried to get her attention, the less interested she seemed. Then he graduated and moved away and he had only ever seen her briefly in the years since. She continued to have no regard for him whatsoever. Even now he wasn't sure what she thought of him, past being a constant annoyance.

He stormed out of the car after her and knocked into Keith coming up the walk. Just what he needed.

"Stay out of the way," he snarled at Keith.

"I never did like you," Keith said. "I can see now that my opinion was well founded. Tell Erin I'll be waiting for her in the car." He spun on his heel and walked off.

Graham went up the steps to where Erin stood on the porch. He got as close to her as he dared. "What you told me will stay between us. I give you my word."

"If you say so." He had a lot to overcome where she was concerned.

The inexplicable need to be near her had him inching closer. "You frustrate the hell out of me, you know that?"

"You aren't doing much more for me either."

He could smell his shower gel on her skin and it brought back the images of her he'd had in his office. He leaned in. "I'm on your side."

"Are you?" She seemed a little out of breath or angry. He couldn't tell.

"I—" One of the tech guys came out of the house and bumped his shoulder, making him realize where he was. He backed away from her. "Stay here. I'll go find your cell phone." He went into the house, concentrating on keeping his steps even and unhurried.

The more time he spent with her, the more he wanted to put his hands on her. Either in an embrace or around her neck, he wasn't sure which. She'd somehow gotten in his head and messed with it. He had to find a way to get her out of it before he forgot why getting involved with her in any way was a bad idea.

The techs had set up their lights, illuminating every corner of the house. Graham found Erin's phone on the floor against the wall outside the kitchen door. He grabbed one of the techs to photograph and catalog it, then took it out to Erin waiting on the porch.

"Here you go."

"Thanks."

"Be at the station by eight tomorrow morning to give your statement."

She went down the steps of the house to Keith without a backwards glance. He thought about calling out a goodbye to her, but figured he'd hit his sarcastic limit with her and would only dig himself in deeper.

So he stood there and watched as Keith came around to open the car door for her. Keith, the high school track star. Keith, the hometown boy who'd stayed. Keith, who didn't say stupid shit to piss her off. Keith, who offered her comfort instead of aggravation. Keith, with the smug look as he got back into his car and drove away with Erin.

Graham wished there was a law against being a self-righteous prick just so he could throw Keith in a cell.

He had to remind himself that it was a good thing she had a boyfriend. She was also a witness in this case, the only witness. And he had no business starting something with her when what had happened in L.A. wasn't completely over.

He watched their taillights until the night swallowed them. A few hearty souls were still camped across the street. The coroner would be bringing the bodies out soon. Graham was sure that's what they were waiting for. He recognized his cousin Willie and lifted a hand in reluctant acknowledgement.

God, he couldn't wait to get out of this town.

He walked into the false florescent nightmare created by the lights the tech guys had set up. Night crime scenes were the worst. Everything was lit up like a movie sound stage, giving it an eerie dreamlike quality. The butcher shop stench of death, mingled with the coppery tang of blood, anchored the scene, ensuring no one present would mistake this for anything other than the horror it was.

He found Pax talking to the coroner in the kitchen. He walked in just as Greg's body bag was being zipped closed. The sudden tightness in his chest caught him off guard. He rubbed at it with the palm of his hand. When he'd left San Rey he'd left everything and everyone behind. Including friends like Greg. Good friends. Somehow taking those friendships with him had seemed impossible at the time. Now it seemed stupid and childish.

He wondered who was left to make Greg's funeral

arrangements before turning his attention to what the coroner was saying to Pax.

"—to the lab, but I can tell you that Na-tabs are prenatal vitamins. My wife took them. If Mrs. Lasiter was prescribed them, she was most likely pregnant. We'll know for sure after the autopsy."

"Can you check paternity against the husband?" Graham asked.

Pax swiveled his head in Graham's direction. "You don't think Greg's the father? Why?"

"I don't know anything for sure," Graham said. "Just covering all the bases."

"We'll check paternity against the husband," the coroner said. "I'll let you know our findings."

"Thanks."

Graham watched them wheel out Greg's, then Deidre's body. He knew well the path his friend's body would take, what the autopsy photos would show, how he'd look pale and waxy on the table, a Y incision carved and stitched into his flesh. Greg should've grown old, died old. If anyone had asked Graham which one of them would be the first to stand over a grave, Graham would've said it would be Greg standing over Graham's. He'd taken risks—too many risks—and survived when more deserving others hadn't. As usual his thoughts drifted to Patricia. Another person who should've grown old and died old. Another grave Graham had to stand over. Another person he'd let down.

Graham shook those thoughts off. That was a bad

road to go down, especially now when there was so much work to do.

He turned to Pax. "Did you get the name of Deidre's doctor from the prescription bottle?"

"I did. I Googled him. His office is in San Luis Obispo."

"Where she lives now." Something nagged at Graham, but he couldn't put his finger on what he was missing. "What's your take on this, Pax?"

Pax puffed up a little, adjusting the weight of his belt. "From the witness's statement and appearances, Greg's death was self-inflicted. Deidre's... it's too soon to tell yet, but my gut says murder/suicide. I'd sure like to know more about why they were getting a divorce. You know, other than what my wife tells me she overheard at the beauty shop."

"What'd your wife hear at the beauty shop?"

"You aren't serious. That's just a bunch of gossiping wives and girlfriends."

"Sometimes there's truth in gossip."

"Well..." Pax began. "Not that I listened or anything, but the talk was that Deidre had plans, was bragging about coming up in the world. And if you tell anybody I passed on rumors from the Clippity-Do-Da, I'll sock you in the teeth."

That jived with what Erin had told him about her vision of the killer.

Graham chuckled. "Hey, man, sometimes police work is dirty work." He clapped Pax on the shoulder. "Keep your ear to the parlor door. I'm counting on you."

"Yeah, right. Next thing, you'll want me to go down

and get a permanent wave so I can record the gossip for you."

Graham pretended to consider it.

"No way I'm stepping foot in that cackle house."

He winked at Pax. "We'll keep that option open just in case. Did the crime scene techs get all the samples I asked for?"

"Yeah. There was one thing they noticed when they moved Deidre's body." He motioned for Graham to come closer. "Deidre had a tattoo right here." He pointed to a spot over his heart. "They said it looked new, still scabby. It was two hands holding a heart." Pax pulled his cell phone from his pocket. "I took a picture of it. Thought you'd want to have a look."

He brought up the photo and handed the phone to Graham. The tattooed design was of a red heart with a crown on top held on either side by hands.

"The Claddagh," Graham said. "Good work."

"The what?"

"An Irish symbol of love, friendship and loyalty. Guys often propose to their girlfriends with a Claddagh ring. My mom has one. How big was the tattoo?"

"About as big as a quarter or half-dollar, why?"

"Just want to put things in perspective. Text me the photo, will you? We'll want to find the shop that did the work. Maybe someone there will remember her and why she got the tattoo."

"Sure."

While Pax worked on sending the text, Graham took another look around the kitchen. The stack of papers on the table and Deidre's purse were gone.

"When you bagged Deidre's purse and the papers on the table, did you move the furniture?" he asked Pax.

Pax looked up from his phone at Graham and then at the table and chair set. He frowned. "No. I only touched the things I bagged. Why?"

"Deidre's purse was on the floor next to the chair on the other side of the table. The divorce papers were on table, facing the chair. Why would she put them there like that if she didn't sit down at the table?"

Pax eyed the chair in question. "It's pushed in."

"Right. Someone pushed the chair in. Could've been Deidre."

"Could've."

"Could've been Greg or someone else."

"No one touched that chair since I got here. If not Deidre or Greg then someone else did it. Maybe a third person? The real killer? This is looking less like murder/suicide, isn't it?"

"Maybe. Too soon to tell. We'll need to talk to everyone the Lasiters knew. Who are Greg and Deidre's next of kin?"

Pax flipped through his notebook. "Greg's brother's in prison, as I'm sure you know."

He didn't know. He should've known. Would everyone assume he'd kept in contact with Greg and the others after all these years?

"He has an uncle on his mother's side in Sacramento," Pax continued. "Deidre has a sister, Denise, who lives in San Luis Obispo and a brother, Darrin, who lives in North Carolina. Her parents, Mr. and Mrs.

Daniel Day, also live in San Luis Obispo. I guess they'd be the next of kin."

"You'd better call Vera and let her know you won't be home for dinner."

Pax closed his notebook with a sad sigh. "I've never done a death notification."

"I have." And he could remember every single detail about every single one. Right down to the noise in the background as he informed parents, siblings and friends that their loved one had died. And now he'd have to tell the family of his old friend that Greg had killed himself and possibly murdered his wife.

5

"What is *happening*?" Erin asked her aunt, whispering into the phone so Keith couldn't overhear from the other room.

"I don't know. Your father thinks... bah! I can't even say it."

"What?"

"He had to pay full price for his lunch today at the Do or Dine and now he's convinced someone is purposely manipulating our abilities."

"He never pays full price. For anything." The only time her father used his ability of suggestion was when money was involved.

"I know! And Tera was his waitress. Her mind's so open to suggestion that her name badge should read: Suggestion Box. Then he went down to Fine's to pick up a few things for his woodworking club and paid full price again! He's so discombobulated he's sure there's some great universal conspiracy cooking."

That would explain why all of their abilities had been affected. But... "By who and how?"

Aunt Cerie sighed into the phone. "I don't know. This whole business has me twisting and turning like a wind chime in a tornado. How are you doing, chicken?"

"I'm okay... I guess."

"You've had a heck of a day. I'm sorry."

"The premonitions are always the worst for me. I hate not being able to change anything."

"If you change even one little thing, you could change everything. You know that."

Erin had heard this lecture before. At least a thousand times. "I know."

"We were given our abilities for a reason. It's a great responsibility. I don't like that your father uses his to get discounts, but at least he doesn't give people the suggestion to give things to him for free. *That* would be irresponsible. It's like if I told Paul Webster that his wife is having an affair with her best friend Gina, I'd be changing the natural order of events. Either Paul will find out or he won't. Although—between you and me— if Paul *did* find out, he'd want to turn the whole thing into a threesome. That guy is into some seriously kinky stuff."

"Aunt Cerie," Erin warned.

She hated it when her aunt told her more than she ever wanted to know about the people around her. Cerie saw nothing wrong with using her ability and wasn't shy about sharing what she learned. She'd supported herself for years off her 'readings', which were really just Cerie telling people what they wanted to hear. Cerie's antics and Donald's uncanny knack for never paying full price fueled the rumors that there was something strange about the Decembers.

"You know I don't want to hear about that kind of stuff." Wait. What if her aunt heard one or both of the Lasiters' thoughts. She might know whom Deidre was having an affair with. Goodness knew Cerie knew about every other affair in town. "Did you ever overhear anything about Greg or his wife?"

"Hmm. Well, there was this one time—"

"Yeah?"

"You know I can't delve into people's brains. I can only overhear what they're thinking at the time."

"I know."

"Well... about a week ago I was in Goldman's Drugs buying some cream for this rash on my side that the doctor can't seem to find the cause of, and two aisles over in personal products I caught the threads of some very interesting thoughts. So I moseyed on over an aisle and listened in, which was quite difficult because I found myself in the incontinence aisle. *That* is not an aisle you want to be seen in."

"No. Of course not. Who was it?"

"Greg Lasiter. He was buying condoms. Only he hadn't bought them in awhile so he was debating what kind to buy. As if there's a choice," Aunt Cerie scoffed. "You buy the lubricated, ribbed for her pleasure ones. Everybody knows that."

Erin dropped her head into her hand and suppressed a groan.

"Anyhoo," Cerie continued, "there he was,

wondering if he should buy the magnum size to impress even though he worried they were too big and would slide off, you know... in the act. And then in the middle of his debate, he gets angry that he has to buy them at all.

"He's ticked off good that his wife's dumped him. Only he's not just mad, he's sad, too. He really loved her and she threw him over all of a sudden. Out of the blue. And he's thinking she's got someone else. He *knows* she's got someone else. Then he picks up two packs of magnum condoms because he's going to burn through them like he's at a college frat party. He's thinking he's going to nail every woman in sight. Every woman who will have him. He runs through several images in his mind. He wasn't very imaginative, but he did have some very complementary thoughts about *your* cleavage."

"Ugh. You could've left that last part out." But it did confirm what she'd seen in her visions. So her ability wasn't totally on the fritz. She had a hard time figuring out if that was a good thing or a bad thing.

"That's about it, really," Aunt Cerie finished.

"What about Deidre Lasiter?"

"Hmm, well, she was a tricky one. I didn't see her all that often, but when I did, her thoughts ran to household things. Grocery lists and the like. If she thought anything about anyone, she never did it around me."

"Can I ask you something?"

"Sure, chicken. Ask me anything."

"When your ability went on the blink as you put it, what did it feel like?"

"Here's the strange thing," Aunt Cerie said. "At first

it just felt like someone flipping a light switch off and on. Then my ability stayed off for longer periods of time, but it came with a sharp pain in my head, like a hammer to the temples."

"How long has it been happening?"

"The off and on thing continued for most of the day, but there was no pattern to it. I didn't think anything of it at first. But it got progressively worse. Then right before you called me, Donald told me he'd been having issues, too. I naturally assumed you might be, as well. I was worried."

"Is that why you told Graham about my ability?" She wasn't sure if she should be angry or relieved about her aunt's meddling. There was something frightening yet freeing about sharing her secret with Graham.

"Yes. And no."

"What does that mean?"

"I didn't want to worry anyone. Especially you."

"I know you." While her aunt collected gossip, she never started it. Something was off here. "What's the real reason?"

Aunt Cerie huffed out a breath. "My mother, your grandmother had some... issues with her ability shortly before she died."

"What kind of *issues*?"

"I never told you because I didn't want to worry you. A few months before her death her abilities started shorting out. Very much like what's been happening to us today. She was never the same after that. I always worried I might fall into the same kind of madness that eventually took her life."

"Do you think what happened to your mother might be happening to us?

"I don't know. Tell me exactly what's been happening to you."

"Normally I have to concentrate to put my ability in action, but today, all of a sudden, the visions starting coming to me without me calling them up. That hasn't happened since I first came into my ability, before I learned to control them. And there was that pain you described."

"This is going to sound strange, but does it feel deliberate to you?"

"What do you mean, deliberate?"

"Like someone is actively messing with your abilities, trying to control them."

It felt *exactly* like that. Like someone or something shoving the visions at her. But that was impossible. Outside of the December family, she didn't know anyone else in San Rey who had abilities.

"Auntie, could there be—" Keith knocked on Erin's bedroom door. She never discussed her and her family's abilities with Keith or anyone else who wasn't a December. Never. "I've got to go," she told her aunt. "But I think there's a possibility here we haven't discussed."

"Come over tomorrow. Your father wants to see you."

Keith opened the bedroom door. "Dinner's ready."

Erin held up a finger for Keith to wait. "I'll stop by after work," she told her aunt.

"Bye, chicken. Take care of yourself."

"You, too, Auntie. Bye."

Erin ended the call and got up from the edge of her bed, smiling at Keith through her new worries. "I'm starving. What are we having?"

"Meatloaf sandwiches. I thought you could use some comfort food."

"Sounds good." She walked into his arms, needing more comfort than food could give her.

He smoothed a hand down her hair. "I have some vacation time coming. Why don't we take a few days and go somewhere? We could go up to Santa Cruz or down to Los Angeles."

She pulled back to look up at him. "I just started my job. I can't take time off right now." He had nice hazel eyes with no wicked dark ring like Graham's. *Where did that thought come from?*

"We could leave on a Friday after work and come back Sunday," he continued to press. "I'd really like to take some time, just the two of us. What do you say?"

She knew what he was getting at, what he wanted. He wanted to take things to a level she wasn't sure she was ready for. The panic started as a low hum, a tightening in her chest. She pressed her face to his shirt and closed her eyes. She could do this. She *should* do this. It was normal for girlfriends to want to have sex with their boyfriends. They'd been dating long enough that his suggestion wasn't out of the norm. Except she couldn't seem to drum up any excitement for it. He was handsome, attractive. Everyone thought so. What was wrong with her? Why wasn't she sexually attracted to him?

Maybe if she just gave it a try, the attraction would come. His heart beat as steady as he was and she found herself agreeing.

"Yes. Okay."

He tightened his arms around her and kissed the top of her head. "I'll make the arrangements. Would you like me to surprise you?"

"I'd like that. I like surprises." She needed someone like him and his normal.

He turned them and guided her toward the kitchen. "Then it's all set. Come and eat your dinner. Later we'll watch some TV or a movie."

She sat down at her small kitchen table. Keith sat across from her. He seemed a little lighter, a little happier. If only she could feel the same. Maybe this vacation would be good for them. She tried to concentrate on the meal and the company, but by the time Keith looked up from his empty plate she'd only eaten half her food and couldn't remember what it tasted like or what they'd been talking about.

"Maybe we should skip that movie," he said.

"I'm sorry. I'm not very good company tonight."

He reached across the table and grabbed her hand, squeezed. "I've been trying to distract you, but I can see it's not working."

"I know you have and I appreciate it."

"I really like you, Erin."

"I like you, too."

"Do you?"

She put her other hand over his and tried for a

smile. "Of course I do. I wouldn't be going away with you if I didn't."

He smiled, his shoulders sagging a little in relief.

"I haven't been a very good girlfriend lately, have I?"

"You've been busy with your new job. I understand. And then with what happened today... You've been through a lot."

"Thanks again for coming to get me. That was very thoughtful of you."

"I'm always thinking of you." He leaned in and gave her a kiss.

"Tell me about your day."

"Nothing to tell." He pulled his hand from hers and stood. "How about dessert? I got the last piece of butter cake from the Do or Dine."

She watched him walk to the refrigerator. He moved with a confident, long-legged grace that had attracted her from the start. He bent over to look into the refrigerator and she was hurled out of her kitchen and dropped into another kitchen. The walls were painted a sunny yellow with a sunflower border. Erin blinked in the sudden brightness. A blueberry pie cooled on the counter, so fresh out of the oven she could smell it.

An older woman Erin recognized as Keith's mother sat at the kitchen table, shucking peas. "I still don't see why it matters. You should just go along as you have been."

Keith pulled his head out of the refrigerator with a can of soda in his hand. He was wearing his Lucky's Bag N Save apron, white button-up shirt and black slacks. His hair was a little longer than it was now. "It'll matter to Erin, so it matters to me."

"Your father isn't going to like this."

"I know."

His mother sighed, took the bowl from her lap, and set it on the table with a thunk. "You're going to be stubborn about this, I can see."

"As stubborn as you."

"Yes, well. You didn't get all my best traits." Keith's mother wiped her hands on a kitchen towel, keeping her gaze on her task. "You're sure you're the responsible party?"

Keith straightened from where he'd been slouching against the refrigerator. "What kind of thing is that to say?"

"The smart thing."

He sat his soda on the counter. "I'm not listening to this." He turned to leave, but his mother's next words stopped him in the doorway.

"I have proof."

He kept his feet planted and tilted his head back to look at the ceiling. "I don't want to hear this."

"But you need to. Don't be a fool."

"A fool?" He turned partially. "It's too late for that."

"Betty saw her meeting another man."

"Mom, don't."

"She didn't see who, but the timing is right enough to give me doubts."

"I'm going to work," Keith blurted. He started for the front door.

His mother got up and followed. "I raised you to be

smart, but since you weren't smart enough stay away from that whore, I'm going to make sure you don't make an even worse mistake."

"Don't call her a whore!"

"Women who sleep around and get pregnant by God knows who are whores. Before you throw away your life on her and her bastard child you're going to ask for a paternity test."

Keith opened the front door and ran down the steps to his car.

"You hear me?" his mother called after him.

Keith jumped into his car, started it and peeled away from the curb, leaving his mother fuming on the porch, hands on her hips.

"Can't keep it in his pants, just like his father," she grumbled under her breath. She went back into the house, picked up the phone, and dialed. "Hello? This is Nancy Collins. I'm calling on behalf of my son. There's something I think you should know—"

Erin sucked in a sharp breath suddenly back in her kitchen. Keith was pulling a pink bakery box out of her refrigerator. Her heart beat so hard the sound filled her head. *Past or future?* She couldn't tell. There'd been nothing in the vision to indicate if what she saw was something that had happened or something that was going to happen. No calendar on the wall, no reference to events she could place. Keith's hair had been longer like it was when they first started dating. She'd been after him to grow it out again. She gripped the edge of the table, trying to get her bearings.

Keith got a couple of forks from a drawer and sat in

his seat. Struggling to make sense of what she'd just experienced, she pasted on a smile and tried to look normal.

He opened the cake box flat. "Should I get some plates?"

"That's... o-okay."

"Is something wrong?"

"No." Her voice was higher than usual. She tried to pitch it lower. "Nothing's wrong."

He frowned, tilting his head to the side. "Are you sure?"

She grabbed a fork and pulled the cake toward her. "Mmm, this looks good." She worked on being normal as she scooped up a bite and pushed it into her mouth.

Keith watched her for a moment, then dug into the cake on his side. "Maybe I should spend the night and look after you."

"No," she answered, too quickly. At his raised brows, she back-pedaled. "I'm just so tired, I don't know what kind of company I'd be."

"I like your company any way I can get it. I'll stop by first thing in the morning then."

"I have to finish giving my statement at the police station and go to work. I wouldn't have any time."

He hunched his shoulders and gave his attention to forking another bite of cake. She'd hurt him, pushed him back yet again.

"Are you seeing someone else?" she blurted out.

His head came up. "What? No. What kind of question is that?"

"I don't know."

He straightened in his chair and looked at her closely. "Are you?"

"No."

He studied her so long she wondered what he could be thinking. "In this town, you'd know if I was seeing someone else." He chuckled, but it sounded forced. "Right?"

"Right."

"We haven't talked about it. I mean I just assumed we were exclusive. There's no one else I want to see."

He looked at her expectantly, his earlier offer to go away together and what it would mean hanging in the air between them.

She thought of Graham and how she'd confided more in him than she'd ever confided in Keith. She shouldn't compare them. Even if she found herself wishing it was Graham she'd agreed to go away with.

"Me either."

He grinned and she couldn't help but return it with a real smile this time. They finished off the cake and talked some more about little things, insignificant things. Not the deepest, darkest secret she carried. Not the horror she'd witnessed earlier. Nothing upsetting or out of the ordinary. It was all so normal, she could scream.

At the door Keith drew her into his arms and kissed her long and deep. He'd been holding out on her. When he lifted his head, she rocked forward on her toes into his chest, catching herself with handfuls of his shirt.

"Sure you don't want me to spend the night?" he asked hopefully.

She didn't have it in her to pretend anymore today. "Another night?"

He kissed her again, a lingering goodbye that had her sighing and leaning against the doorway as she watched him walk to his car. He really was cute and if he kept kissing her like that, she might forget she wasn't attracted to him physically. He waved to her as he pulled away from the curb. She closed the door, grinning like a smitten teenager. Maybe the trip would be just what they needed.

Remembering her earlier vision, she dropped the smile. Had it been a premonition or a scene from the recent past? She moved to a chair and sat down. Closing her eyes, she drew up the scene in the sunny-yellow kitchen again. Keith had mentioned her name in the beginning... something about *it* mattering to her. But what? It was clear Keith had gotten someone pregnant or thought he had. Someone who had been sleeping with another man. Erin had only been dating Keith for a few months, so if this was the recent past, then he had some explaining to do.

If this was the future...

She didn't want to think about that, because in the future she'd seen, Keith was going to get someone pregnant, someone who was cheating on him. Either Erin was going to be cheated on or she was going to cheat. If she was going to cheat, whom was she going to cheat with? And if she was the cheater, then she was the one who was going to end up pregnant. Again her thoughts drifted toward Graham.

The whole thing made her forehead hurt. She suddenly wished for her aunt's ability. She'd just skim Keith's thoughts and then she'd know. Right now the only thing she knew for sure was that she was going to Goldman's Drugs tomorrow to double up on her birth control.

And hope she wasn't somehow messing with the future.

6

Graham dragged his tired ass up the steps of his parents' house. It was after midnight, but he knew his dad would be waiting in his study. At least the rain had finally stopped. He let himself in with his key and closed the door quietly behind him. He didn't want to wake his mother sleeping upstairs. Creeping down the dark hall, relying on decades of memory, Graham remembered other times he'd tried to sneak into the house, only to find his father waiting for him. Nothing happened in this house or this town that Ham Doran didn't know about.

A thin bar of light showed under the bottom of the study door. He'd told his pop he'd talk things over later, but now that it was later—he checked his phone —*much* later, all Graham wanted was a drink, a shower, and to fall face down in bed. But he'd made a promise. He'd gotten out of the habit of keeping his promises in L.A. If he went back to L.A. he wouldn't go back to being the man he was when he'd left. He let out an exhausted sigh and knocked, then let himself into his dad's study.

Ham looked up from the papers he'd been reading at his desk. "Hello, son." He opened a drawer and tucked the papers inside, closing it afterward. "Late night."

Graham dropped into the chair across the desk from his father. "Helluva a day, followed by a bitch of a night."

Ham opened another drawer and pulled out a bottle of whiskey. "Watch your mouth," he admonished, rummaging around in the drawer until he came up with two paper cups. He poured an inch of whiskey in each, then handed one to Graham. "You're under my roof, my rules."

"Yes, sir." Some things never changed. Graham took a sip that burned so good he took another. "Pax and I were on standby when Sacramento P.D. informed Greg's uncle of his nephew's death, then we drove out to San Luis Obispo to notify Deidre Lasiter's parents."

Ham sat back in his chair, propping his cup on his stomach. "I had to do that once. Notify next of kin. Remember when Fred Sparks had a heart attack under Judy Lindberg's Corolla right there in his repair shop?" Ham shook his head. "When they rolled him out from under, the wrench he was using was still in his hand. Went out to notify Freda of Fred's death myself. She took it well. Married Sam Streetah the next week. Sold the repair shop and moved to Antigua. Now her name's Freda Streetah from Antigua." He pointed a finger at Graham's snicker. "That's all true as far as you know."

Graham's chuckle died slowly. "I wish Deidre's parents had taken it as well." He took another drink of whiskey. "According to the Days, Deidre was pregnant with their first grandchild when she died." He finished the last sip and stared at the bottom of the empty cup. "They'd bought some baby things already."

Ham unscrewed the cap on the whiskey and splashed some into his cup. He offered Graham more with a tilt of the bottle. Graham shook his head. He didn't need his thoughts anymore addled.

"That's rough," Ham said.

"Yeah. I'm having the baby, fetus, whatever, tested against Greg's DNA for paternity."

"What makes you think it's not Greg's?"

"It's standard." Graham lied and counted this as the second time in his whole life he'd ever lied to his father. He suddenly wished he'd accepted that second drink.

"Standard," Ham mumbled.

Graham shifted in his seat. "I was hoping you could give me some background on the Lasiters. Things that might have come to your attention from a law enforcement

standpoint. Any domestic violence, DUI, disturbing the peace or anything like that I should know about?"

"We don't get much of any of that around here. San Rey's been a peaceful town until today. You know that."

"I just thought of it as boring growing up," Graham said.

"As long as a Doran's been sheriff, this town's been a safe place to live."

"That's an old superstition."

Ham moved his hand in a think-what-you-want motion.

"You don't seriously believe that, do you?" Graham asked.

"I don't have to. It got me reelected every term and you elected in my place. And someday if you ever shave your beard, get a wife, and act like you give a darn, it'll get your son elected sheriff, too. That's the way of it."

"Pop, you know I'm only filling in until Adam gets home. I've got a job, a home, a life in Los Angeles that I want to get back to." Or more like a life he wanted to rebuild in L.A.

"Your brother's a second son. Only first sons become sheriff, you know *that*. Besides, Adam signed up for another tour of duty. He's not coming home any time soon."

"Son of a—"

"I told you to watch your mouth in my house," Ham growled. Ham could still be intimidating, Graham realized with surprise.

Graham slid to the front of his chair and slammed his empty cup on the desk, crumpling it. "When did this happen?"

"About three months ago."

"You let me think...all the time you were in the hospital and through that farce of an election, you let me think this whole thing was temporary."

He'd gone along with it to placate his father. He didn't think Ham's health could take a lot of pushback at the time. Stepping in temporarily also gave Graham time to figure his own shit out and if he should go back to L.A. or someplace else where his past didn't trail out behind him. He'd thought he had an out. But now...

Graham pushed to his feet and leaned across the desk. "You tricked me."

"I didn't do anything of the sort. You sit down and listen." Ham glared at his son until Graham dropped back into his seat with a huff. "You have a responsibility to me, this family, and this town." Ham pointed at Graham. "You're a Doran. It's high time you lived up to your heritage."

Graham rubbed a finger across his bearded chin, looking everywhere but at his father. Trapped. He was well and truly trapped. His father had boxed him in, knowing it was always Graham's plan to leave this godforsaken town. Ham knew that Graham wasn't going to stay. *Son of a mother-fucking bitch!*

"When you come to accept what is, you'll see I'm right," Ham said.

"Pax should have been elected sheriff. He's put in the time and he already lives here. He's a good man."

"Pax isn't a Doran. Now, that's the end of it."

And the sad thing was, his father was right. This was the end of it. The end of his career in the LAPD narcotics squad. The end of his life being his. He'd thought almost losing his father had been bad. This was ten times worse. Almost losing something was nothing like *actually* losing it.

"What did your witness say in her statement?" Ham asked.

Graham dropped heavily back into his chair. Old resentments rose up, threatening to choke him. He'd thought by leaving, things would change, his father would change. But nothing changed in a town that stayed the same year after year, decade after decade, generation after generation. By returning he'd been sucked back into the expectations and responsibilities he'd run from. He doubted he'd be able to escape a second time. Maybe this was his punishment for what had happened in L.A. with Patricia. Maybe this was his comeuppance. God knew he deserved this and more. He couldn't have chosen a more ironic penance than this.

"Pretty much what I already told you." Graham couldn't keep the bitterness out of his tone. "She's not giving her formal statement until tomorrow. Do you mind if I go? It's late."

"Sure, son."

Graham stood. "Well, good-night." He started for the door, his tread heavy.

"Graham?" He looked back at his father. "It's good to have you home."

He nodded and left the study, wishing he could escape responsibility as easily. He'd counted on his father to be sheriff until Adam came home. Had hoped his move to Los Angeles would have been enough, but here he was, right back where he didn't want to be.

The sea wind hit him full force, a briny slap in the face. He jogged to his car and climbed in, needing to get the hell out of there. He was trapped. Trapped by tradition and familial expectations. Trapped in a town that ate at his soul. He hated the confines of small town life, the small minds and big mouths. He could almost feel it closing in on him, suffocating him. He didn't belong here and he couldn't quite see his way back to L.A. and the memories that waited for him there.

He sped down the deserted streets, passing memories along the way. The corner where he'd crashed his first bike. The diner where he'd had his first date. The baseball field where he'd played Little League. He knew the name of the family that lived in almost every house he passed. He knew which businesses were new and which had been around for generations, transitioning from one family member to the next.

He'd never thought of his family's legacy as anything other than a burden, a duty to escape from, like mowing the lawn or hauling out the trash. His father spoke of it as though it was an honor. He wished he felt the same. He would always fail his father in that way. His father's disappointment in him had become a near tangible thing he brushed and bumped up against almost constantly. He didn't know how to be the son his father wanted him to be.

He stopped his car and suddenly realized he'd come to the bluffs, the highest point in San Rey. The muffled roar of the sea dashing on the rocks below drew him out of the car. He'd often come here as a teenager to think or try to get in some girl's pants. Forgoing the bench, he stood at the railing and looked out over the night-blackened ocean. There was something about the rhythmic ebb and flow of the tide that soothed him. It was constant, dependable. He pulled in a deep breath and tilted his face into the misty breeze, closing his eyes. If only he could be like the waves, coming and going as he pleased.

After several steadying moments, he opened his eyes and glanced down at the rocks below. Maybe he was more like the rocks than the water. A static thing that life pounded and crashed against, trying to wear down. It was colder here with nothing to block the wind. Graham didn't mind the cold. It matched his mood. He stayed at the railing, his body tense against the chill, until his eyeballs hurt and his hands went numb. He jammed them in his pockets and turned to go back to his car. The outline of a figure sitting on the bench startled him. He reached for his weapon by habit, his heart banging hard against his ribcage, then halted the motion when recognition hit.

Her. What was *she* doing here?

"Sorry. I was trying not to disturb you," Erin said, her voice as thin and wispy as the ocean breeze.

He made his way over, forgetting the cold and the reasons he had for leaving. He stopped in front of her. "What are you doing out here?"

"Probably the same thing as you."

"I doubt that."

She scooted over, making a motion for him to sit beside her. He did.

"I came to clear my head," she said, looking out over the black ocean. "Too many clouds to see the moon tonight, but it's there."

"Do you come here often?"

She laughed and it did something funny to his insides. "That sounds like a bad pick up line."

"I don't really have any good ones. *Wanna see my gun* is about as good as it gets."

She looked at him, leaning back a little. "That *is* awful."

"Told you."

"I suppose you don't need pick up lines with those eyes, do you?"

She liked his eyes? That thought made him cheerier than he'd been all day. Hell, all week. Maybe all month.

She returned her gaze to the dark sky. "Can't see any stars either. That's my favorite thing about coming out here at night. There are so many stars."

He stole that moment to look at her profile, shadowed and uninhibited. She'd tucked her hair into a knit cap and wrapped a scarf around her neck, framing her face as though it was a picture. There was something so very honest and forthright about her.

"How do you stand it?" The words fell out before he knew he was going to say them.

She tilted her head and looked at him. "What?"

"This town."

"What do you mean?"

"The smallness."

"That's one of the things I like most about it. It's quaint."

"Haven't you ever wanted to be anonymous? To be able to tell somebody something about yourself without them already knowing everything about you and your family?"

"Ah," she said with a small, sad smile. "Our families are famous in this town for very different reasons."

"Just my point. Wouldn't it be nice to walk into a room and not carry generations of your family's baggage?"

"At least your baggage matches. Mine is mismatched and Duct-taped together." Her smile flattened and her expression turned brooding. "You fit in. I never have."

"Fitting in isn't belonging."

"For me it is."

Her words hit him hard, making him feel like the world's biggest dumb ass. Here he was complaining about the respect his family's legacy afforded him, while hers set her apart.

"I'm sorry," he said.

Hitching a shoulder, she jerked her gaze away. "Nothing for you to be sorry about."

He racked his brain for words to fill the long, awkward silence that followed. None came. He could only stare at her profile and wonder what it would be like if their roles were reversed. If he were the outcast free to leave any time he wanted and she was the one anchored to the community by generations of service.

"I can see how your family's legacy might feel strangling," she said, breaking into the quiet. "It's like a rich people problem."

"What do you mean?"

"Having money doesn't make your problems go away. It brings a whole new set of problems, but it also brings more choices."

"My problem leaves me no choice," he said.

"Not true. You could *choose* to not see it as a problem."

"Accept it, you mean? Just give in?"

"No. Give over to it."

Give over to it. She was talking about something he didn't know anything about, a different kind of acceptance. But wasn't that just a fancy word for giving in?

He shook his head. "I don't have your optimism."

"It's not optimism. Happiness can be as simple as making a decision."

"If it's that simple, why haven't you put it into practice?"

"Who says I'm not happy?"

"You did."

She looked at her lap where she'd twisted the fringe of her scarf around her finger. "I'm happy."

Her tone told a different story. He dropped the subject rather than upset her more.

"I used to bring girls up here sometimes." He pointed to where the bluffs bent back before curving around again. "Right over there is a group of trees with perfect camouflage. A blanket, an illicit bottle of cheap alcohol, and a willing girl in the moonlight is a beautiful thing."

"Yeah, Susie Philpot swore she saw a shooting star at the exact moment you took her virginity."

He couldn't help grinning in surprise. "Oh, yeah?"

"Susie set us all up for disappointment. There were no shooting stars or fireworks when I lost mine."

"That's because you didn't lose it to me," he joked.

She chuckled. "No, I certainly didn't. All I got was a big ole *that's it?* and a sticky mess to clean up."

He barked out a laugh that sounded old and little used. She watched him with a strange awed look on her face.

"What?" Self-consciousness made him ask a little too defensively.

"You should laugh more. It completely changes your face. And you get these little laugh lines right here." She touched a finger to the corner of his eye. "Very sexy, like a movie star."

"A movie star? I don't think so. But I'll take the very sexy part."

"Your modesty borders on annoying."

She was smiling up at him and he forgot the cold, forgot the surf pounding the rocks below, and the distant bark of sea lions. Forgot why kissing her was such a bad idea as he leaned forward, his gaze dropping to her mouth. She put a hand on his chest and he thought for a moment she might shove him back. Instead she fisted the lapel of his jacket and pulled him the rest of the way toward her.

"This is probably a bad idea," he murmured and instantly felt her grip change, pushing him away. The exact opposite of what he wanted. Or maybe the very thing he wanted. Kissing a local girl was probably not the smartest thing he could do right now.

"You're right." She leapt up and backed away from him. "I can't do this."

He caught himself with a palm on the bench

seconds before he face planted. "What the hell just happened?" he said more to himself than to her.

"I have a boyfriend," she asserted.

"He's not here now."

"That's not... It doesn't matter. We're committed."

"Somebody should be committed and I think it's me." *Why was he trying to talk her into what he'd just talked her out of?* He shook his head. *And why couldn't he keep his big, freaking mouth shut?*

She started backing away from him toward the staired path that wound down to town. "I should go."

"Let me drive you home at least."

"No need. My house isn't far."

He stood and followed her. "Erin. Let me drive you."

ERIN KNEW if she stayed one more moment under the moonless sky with Graham Doran she'd do more than temporarily forget she had a boyfriend. She needed to leave. Now.

"I don't think that's a good idea," she said, scrambling backward.

Her foot caught on a rock. She teetered at the top of the stairs, arms pinwheeling. Time slowed. The sky rushed across her vision. Graham dashed forward. He grabbed her, pulling her from the edge so suddenly her head snapped forward. She gripped him roughly, her heart pounding so hard she couldn't speak. The sensation of falling stayed with her and she didn't think she'd be able to stand without him.

"Jesus God," he breathed, clutching her closer. "You scared the shit out of me."

"Me, too."

"Erin—"

She cut off his words with the firm press of her lips. His surprised oomph morphed into a low growl as he changed the angle of the kiss, pulling her closer still. His lips were cool from the night air, making his mouth seem even hotter. She wound her arms around his neck and threaded her fingers into his hair. His hand slid down to her backside, bringing her into him. She pressed closer, rocking against him. He felt so good. It all felt so damn good. She'd wanted this from the moment he'd sat down on the bench next to her.

He trailed his lips along her jaw, murmuring words she didn't understand, but knew the meaning of. In answer, she dragged his mouth back to hers. She felt the brush of his thumb on the underside of her jaw. She was hot from him and cold from the night air and wet where she wanted him. The sensations built, one piling on the other until she was throbbing with need.

He backed her against a tree. Her clothing caught on the rough bark, pinning her between it and him. He was so hot and hard against her. The rain began in fat drops, but she didn't care. He kept kissing her, his hands moving lazily over her.

Breaking their kiss, his mouth near her ear, he made his offer again, giving it a whole new meaning. "Let me take you home."

"Yes."

Lightning flashed, followed by the loud clap of thunder. He gave her a hard kiss and wrapped an arm around her. The clouds opened, unleashing their burden in sheets. Hunching under the onslaught, they ran to Graham's car, laughing. She was still laughing when Graham deposited her in the seat and ran around the car. He slid in on his side, slamming the door behind him. Their laughter died in the close confines of the car. Rain bulleted the roof, thunder roared overhead.

"Do you know how long I've wanted to do that?" he asked, a little out of breath.

"What?"

"Kiss you." His words settled around them, changing the mood in increments.

"No." Her response was a breath of sound. How *would* she know? He'd hardly acknowledged her until today and when he did well, she didn't even think he liked her.

She could just make out the shape of his features in the darkened car, but couldn't see his eyes. Focusing on his mouth, she watched as they formed the words she half longed for, half dreaded hearing.

"Feels like forever."

"Your lips are softer than I imagined they'd be," she quietly confessed.

Holding her hand, he kissed the back of it. This felt too intimate, too much like they were starting something that couldn't be stopped. She wasn't free to start up something with Graham or anyone else.

"Can you take me home now?" she asked.

He squeezed her hand, taking her words the wrong way.

"I'm tired," she added, making her meaning clear. "It's been a difficult day."

He took her chin in his hand and turned her toward him. He searched her face for a minute that felt like an hour. She didn't know what he saw or if he could even see anything at all. Nodding slowly, he released her. He started the engine and shifted into gear, beginning their journey down the hill.

She broke the silence now and then to direct him to her house. He kept his eyes on the road and didn't comment. Finally he pulled up to the curb of her small Craftsman bungalow and killed the engine.

"Thanks for the ride." She reached for the door handle.

"I don't like him."

"Who?"

"The Jolly Green Grocer."

"You don't have to like him."

"I don't think you like him either." He shifted in his seat, angling toward her. "Do you?"

"I like him." She put as much enthusiasm in her words as she could muster with the feel of Graham's body still imprinted on hers and his smell wrapped around her.

"Very convincing. Did you know you have a tell?"

"Like in poker?

"Why are you with him if you don't like him?"

"Thanks again for the ride."

She made to leave, but he reached across her and

clamped his hand over hers. "Answer my question and you can go."

Pulling her hand out from under his, she pressed back against the seat as far as she could, evading his touch. "Why do you care?"

"Just tell me. What is it, the apron? The commanding way he handles melons?"

"Stop mocking him," she defended.

He leaned in, his voice dropping to that seductive growl she had trouble resisting. "Come on, tell me."

His eyes glinted dark and mesmerizing and once again she found herself falling down his rabbit hole of persuasion. She wanted to tell him about her doubts, her inability to feel anything more than friendship toward Keith. She wanted to move closer to Graham and touch him the way she couldn't touch Keith. Graham seemed to understand her in a way Keith didn't. The way Keith couldn't. Graham was the only other person besides her family who knew about her ability. And she was glad she'd told him about it. He accepted it, accepted her.

"I do like him." She couldn't seem to stop defending Keith to Graham. The fault of their relationship lay with her, not Keith. She wanted Graham to understand that. "He's good to me. We have a nice time together."

"But?" he prodded.

"But...I just wish I was more attracted to him. You know, physically. He's handsome. Everyone thinks so."

He frowned. "I'm still not getting why you're with him."

"He coaches Little League. His store donates the

food for the spring carnival every year because he arranges it. He's on the committee to keep San Rey clean. He—"

"Belongs," Graham finished. "I get it. He's got what you want."

"And what is it you think I want?"

"Acceptance by osmosis."

"It's not like that." But it was *exactly* like that. Being with Keith gave her a credibility she lacked on her own. His acceptance of her should've translated to acceptance of town. Should've, but didn't.

He sat back in his seat, suddenly looking tired. "I'll see you in the morning."

His abrupt dismissal stung. She should've been glad to be away from him and his gaze that saw too much, away from his questions that made her look too closely at her life and the lies she'd told herself trying to reinvent it.

"Thanks again for the ride," she said, opening the door. "Good-night."

She climbed out of the car and closed the door behind her without looking back. She could feel his gaze on her all the way up her front steps. He didn't pull away from the curb until she'd gotten safely inside, lights on, door locked behind her.

It wasn't until later, just before she drifted off to sleep, that she realized what she'd done by kissing Graham. Keith had never kissed her like that. He never would. She'd never feel—in a thousand kisses with Keith—what she felt in that one kiss with Graham Doran.

7

E rin arrived at the police station promptly at eight only to find Graham hadn't yet come down from his apartment upstairs. This unfortunate turn of events meant that she'd have to make small talk with Mabel while she waited. Except with Mabel, the talking was never small. It was strained, and stretched more horribly than Mabel's girdle elastic.

"You know I'm not one to talk," Mabel was saying, her towering strawberry blond beehive wobbling. "But did you see that new sports car Reverend James bought? If I were Mrs. Reverend James I'd've made him turn around and take it right on back to the dealer." She put her hand to the corner of her coral-painted mouth as an aside. "The way I hear it, the good reverend's been passing the plate to the Unitarian lady pastor over in Santa Maria. If you know what I mean."

Erin bit back a groan, turning a polite smile on

Mabel. "Did Graham say when he'd be down? I have to get to work."

The door opened and swung wide, smacking against the wall. Elmer Farnsworth III shuffled over the threshold. "Sorry. Door got away from me."

Elmer was one more way in which Keith tried and Erin failed him. Keith had thought ahead and hired a lawyer, trying to protect her, but the effort felt like another obligation she owed Keith.

"Oh, don't you worry about that, Elmer," Mabel said as she got up from her desk and pushed the door closed against the wind. "Happens all the time after a storm."

"I'm here after my client... oh, there you are, Eileen," Elmer said.

"It's Erin," Erin corrected.

"Right. That's what I said. Point me to the restroom, will ya, Mabel?"

Mabel pointed. "Down the hall to your right."

As soon as Mabel stepped away from it, the door crashed opened again. Jessica stomped, then wiped her shoes on the doormat before coming inside. "Sorry, Mabel." She hefted the tray of coffee cups in her hands. "My hands were full. They didn't have the blueberry muffin you wanted so I got you bran. Hello, Erin. Isn't Sheriff Doran down yet?"

Mabel closed the door behind Jessica. "No, and I haven't heard a peep out of him. I was just about to call up."

"Oh, no. Don't do that," Jessica said, setting her burden down on her desk. "I'll go see if he's awake."

As soon as Jessica disappeared from view, Mabel

started up again. "That one there." She gestured toward the direction Jessica had gone. "Is angling to be Mrs. Sheriff Doran. I bet she's hoping to catch him in the shower or just out of it. That would be a sight, wouldn't it?"

Erin's mouth fell open. She'd heard the rumors about Jessica pursuing Graham. As far as she knew they were just that—rumors. Until now.

Mabel blathered on, but Erin's mind went to what was happening upstairs. Of Graham in the shower. Naked. She lost all track of what Mabel was saying. It wasn't like Mabel needed an audience anyway.

After last night, Erin knew she was on dangerous ground, imagining Graham without clothes. But the images were so very vivid. And then...boom. She was there. Literally in the shower with Graham. Mabel's voice was gone, replaced with the sounds of water hitting tile and rushing down the drain. Her consciousness hovered just inside the scene, looking down.

Steam billowed, hazing her view. The scent of shampoo and soap hung in the air. Hanging his head, Graham let the water spill over his back. His dark hair was matted against his skull, water trickling down his face to drip off the clean-shaven cleft in his chin. He looked tired, worn down.

Past or Future?

Erin didn't even try to keep her gaze from wandering over his still form or from admiring the contours of his body as the water slithered like a loving hand over his flesh. She reached out to touch, her fingers skimming through him. Neither of them was real. They were nothing more than two beams of light passing through one another. But she ran her hands over his image anyway, imagining how his skin would feel, how warm and slick it would be. How it would feel to press her body to his, the slip and slide of skin on skin.

He dipped his head back, letting the water hit his scalp. She traced a finger over the column of his throat, following it with her lips...

A door banged closed, bringing Erin crashing back to the present. She shook her head, trying to clear the images from her brain. Not again. Was her ability even hers to control anymore?

Footsteps thundered on the stairs. Mabel put a hand to her heart, her mouth open mid-harangue. Jessica barreled into the room. A door opened above.

"Don't ever come up here again!" Graham shouted, punctuating his point by slamming the door.

Jessica skidded to a halt behind Mabel's chair as though she was hiding behind her mommy.

"What the devil did you do, Jessica?" Mabel asked.

Her chest puffing, Jessica's lips slowly curved into a smile that matched the wicked look in her eyes. "Answering the age-old question," she said.

Mabel patted the ample flesh pillowing her chest. "And what in the world would that be? How to scare an old woman half to death?"

Jessica shook her head, her grin growing. "Boxers or briefs?"

"You don't say?" Mabel craned her neck as though she could see up the stairs for herself. "And?"

"Neither. At least not when he sleeps," Jessica answered, looking for all the world as though she'd discovered the cure for cancer or something.

Jealousy, hot and seething, burned through Erin. She wanted to smack the superior look off Jessica's pretty face. If only she could clamp her hand over Jessica's mouth to keep her from describing in great detail what Erin had only seen in her vision.

"He has a tattoo," Jessica said smugly. "On his left shoulder blade. Some kind of Chinese symbol. What I wouldn't give to trace it with my tongue." She sighed dramatically.

"Jessica Ann Conway!" Mabel exclaimed, blushing all the way to her white roots. "You naughty thing."

"Oh, come on, Mabel," Jessica said, tucking a strand of blond hair behind one ear. "I'm sure you've had your share of impure thoughts about our sexy sheriff. I bet Erin has too. Haven't you?"

Oh, yes. "No."

Jessica crossed her arms over her chest and gave Erin a mocking look. "Then why are you blushing?"

Erin touched fingertips to her flaming cheek. "I'm not."

"You're embarrassing her," Mabel said. "Besides, what would Erin be doing lusting after the sheriff when she's got such a handsome boyfriend like Keith?"

"As my grammie says, just because you've already ordered dinner doesn't mean you still can't look at the menu." Jessica's naughty smile flared up again. "And what a fine menu it is. I'll take one of everything."

"Jessica!" Mabel admonished.

"Did Graham say when he'd be down?" Erin asked, trying to change the subject.

Jessica narrowed her eyes. "Graham? Don't you mean Sheriff Doran?"

The door down the hall opened and Elmer hobbled into view, his cane thumping against the wood floor. "I wouldn't go in there for a while if I was you," he said, waving a hand in front of his face.

Jessica settled at her desk with a sigh. "If only he was a back sleeper. I would've gotten to see *all* the goods."

"Your mother would box your ears if she heard you talking about the sheriff like that," Mabel said without any heat, a rosy glow tinting her cheeks. "You didn't happen to take a picture with your phone, did you?"

"Mabel!" Jessica echoed Mabel's tone. "I'm shocked!" She snapped her fingers. "Wish I'd thought of it."

Elmer finally made it across the room and sat down next to Erin. "I used to give the ladies a time myself when I was the sheriff's age. That is, until Ruth snared me in her net. God rest her."

"Did *the sheriff* say when he'd be down?" Erin asked again. "I really do have to get to work."

"Probably be another ten minutes or so," Mabel answered. "Not like he has to take the time to shave."

"I like the scruff. It's sexy," Jessica said.

So did Erin. And the way his soft beard had felt against her skin as he'd kissed her. She flushed again for an entirely different reason.

The phone on Mabel's desk rang. "Sheriff's office...

A what?" She scrambled around on her desk before finally coming up with a pen and paper. "Say that again, Ned. Uh-huh. And you're sure that's where you put it?"

Jessica scooted her rolling chair over to Mabel's desk to read what Mabel was writing. "Auto theft? Who'd want to steal Ned Jenkins' Cadillac? That thing's older than me." Mabel scribbled some more, then underlined something she wrote, pointing it out for Jessica to read. "Computer, jewelry, stereo... whoa. A break-in? Are you sure Ned hasn't been drinking and pawning again?"

Mabel clamped a hand over the mouthpiece. "Keep your voice down. He can hear you."

Jessica crab-walked her chair back to her desk, shaking her head. "Must be a full moon or something. A murder/suicide and now a break-in. Nothing *ever* happens around here and then within twenty four hours—whammo—crime spree."

Mabel's other line rang. She stared at it as though it was a live wire, then turned to Jessica. Pointing at the blinking light, she mouthed *line two?*

Jessica's brows shot up her forehead. "I didn't even know that line worked."

"Can you hold on for a moment, Ned? I have a call on the other line." Mabel said the last sentence as though the devil himself was calling in from hell. She punched the hold button, took a deep breath, then pressed the blinking second line. "Sheriff's office. A streaker," she gasped, clasping a hand to her chest. "Running down Main Street?"

Jessica rolled back over to Mabel's desk. "Who is it? Who's streaking?"

"I'll send a deputy to take care of it," Mabel said, her face reflecting the shock Erin felt. Mabel hung up the phone. "A streaker. We never even had one when they were fashionable."

"Who's the streaker?" Jessica asked as Mabel's second line flashed again.

"Chris Farnsworth." Mabel cast Elmer an uncomfortable look. "You' better go down there, Elmer. Maybe you could help Pax subdue your grandson and talk him into putting his clothes back on." She pressed line two with even more trepidation than before. "Sheriff's office."

Jessica leaned close to Mabel. "What's happened now?"

"Yes, we know," Mabel said into the phone. "It's already been called in. A deputy will be there shortly." She hung up the phone only to have the line light up again. "If that call is about the streaker, they can just hold their horses. Shesh."

"I can't imagine what would possess that boy to do such a foolish thing," Elmer said, struggling to get his feet under him.

Jessica popped up out of her chair, flashing a mischievous grin. "I'll walk you over to Main Street, Elmer."

Erin assisted Elmer to the door where Jessica was already putting her coat on. She ignored Erin, looking through her to Elmer.

"I'll have my cell phone ready this time, you know

in case you need me," she told Mabel with a wink, closing the door behind her and Elmer.

Erin rolled her shoulders, some of her tension leaving with Jessica. *Where was Graham?* She checked the time again. She was going to be later than she'd told her boss she'd be. Ramie had informed her on the phone the night before how disappointed he was in her that she hadn't gotten the check from Greg. He didn't hide his annoyance when she told him she was going be late to work the next morning so she could give her statement to the police. The last thing Ramie wanted was bad publicity for his company. He was very unhappy about her involvement in Greg and Deidre's deaths. She'd be lucky if she still had a job at the end of the day.

"The sight of Chris Farnsworth buck naked, running down Main Street is not a sight I want to see," Mabel said. "I changed that boy's diapers. I've seen all of his privates I ever want to see." She picked up a headset and put it on. "Pax. Come in."

While Mabel gave Pax the particulars of Chris Farnsworth's marathon down Main Street, Erin wondered what in the world was happening in San Rey. Three crimes in twenty-four hours. She couldn't recall three crimes in a year, let alone a day. Combined with her highjacked ability and the issues her aunt and father were having, there was definitely something strange going on. *But what did it mean?*

The door opened at the top of the stairs. Graham's heavy tread announced him before Erin saw him. Man, the first hit of him was the most potent. A new flush crept up her cheeks, a combination of what had happened between them the night before and her vision of him in the shower.

"Hey," he said without eye contact, making a beeline for the tray of coffees on Jessica's desk.

"Hey," Erin answered back in the same effortless tone.

Mabel pulled her headset back on and pressed the button for line two. "Sheriff's office."

"What's going on?" Graham asked.

"It seems as though San Rey's having a bit of a crime spree." Erin motioned toward Mabel. "Mabel's had four calls in the twenty minutes I've been here."

"That phone doesn't ring four times in a week." Graham took his coffee to Mabel's desk. He waited for her to finish the third streaker complaint, his expression growing more and more confused. "Did you just say streaker?" he asked Mabel.

"I'm afraid so. Chris Farnsworth decided to take a stroll down Main Street wearing the suit he was born in. Although I'm pretty sure that boy wasn't born painted San Rey High's colors. Seems he's celebrating the football team's win last night. In a really big, really illegal way. I sent Pax over to throw a blanket on him or something."

Shaking his head, Graham chuckled. "Kids."

"I wish that was all," Mabel said. "Oh, shoot! Ned Jenkins is still on line one." She punched the blinking line. "Sorry, Ned. We're having a busy morning here. I'll send the sheriff himself on over to take a report. Say howdy to Yvette for me. Okay, will do. Bye."

"What's Ned calling about?" Graham asked.

"A break-in," Mabel said. "Somebody made off with his Cadillac and a bunch of other stuff. He's really teed off."

"A break-in? In San Rey? I don't believe it. You'd better call Yvette and make sure he didn't take a trip to the pawnshop he doesn't want her to know about."

"He insists he wasn't drinking last night, Graham. And I believe him. He sounded Monday morning sober, not Friday night drunk. And I'd know the difference, having been married to him once upon a time."

He considered her. "I guess you would. Why don't you send Pax over there when he's done? I have to take Erin's statement."

"Elmer went down with Jessica to see if he can't help get Chris under control."

Graham had started toward his office, then turned back at the mention of Jessica's name. "That's another thing. If that girl steps one foot on those stairs again, I'm firing her. I don't care if she is your niece."

"Technically she's not my niece anymore since I divorced her no good, dirty, rotten uncle," Mabel pointed out. "That was two husbands ago. No, three. I forgot about Stiffless Stan who is truly forgettable. Couldn't even get it up half mast if you know—"

"Whatever," Graham cut in, frustration edging the word. "Just keep Jessica out of my apartment."

"I really need to get to work," Erin said. "When can we reschedule?"

"We're not rescheduling," he told her, then addressed Mabel. "Call Jessica and tell her to get Elmer back down here. And tell her to get her butt in her chair where it belongs. The city's not paying her to take pictures of naked men on Main Street so she can text them to her friends."

Just then Mabel's cell phone beeped. She looked at the screen and let out a squeak before pressing it face down on the top of her desk. "How'd you know she was going to do that?"

"I'm a goddamned rocket scientist," Graham muttered as he headed toward his office. He paused in the doorway. "Come in, Erin. We can get a head start and get you to work that much sooner. Send Elmer in when he gets here," he told Mabel.

"Sure thing, boss," she responded, turning back to her phone and the two new incoming calls.

Erin followed Graham, nervous about being alone with him. After the way they'd left things last night, she wasn't sure where things stood between them. Would they go back to being little more than acquaintances or would their changed relationship carry over into the new day?

Graham waited for her to enter his office, then closed the door behind her. "Goddamned small town," he mumbled to himself, then to her. "Have a seat while I get set up. I'll keep it brief so you can be on your way."

His curt business tone threw her for a moment, but then what did she expect? She'd set the terms and boundaries of their relationship last night. He was only following them. This is what she wanted. She had no right to the disappointment that crept over her.

"Thank you."

He didn't respond as he gathered a digital recorder and small spiral bound notebook. He settled at his desk and flipped through the notebook, making notes on another sheet of paper. She focused on the room rather than on Graham where her gaze seemed to want to fix.

There was really nothing to it, she realized with some surprise. She hadn't paid much attention the night before, but its utter starkness was depressing. There were no personal photos unless she counted the portraits of the five Sheriff Dorans that had come before, hanging on the wall behind him. No certificates, no doodads on the desktop, no funny coffee mug or breath mints... nothing to give away whom the office belonged to.

He could drop everything and leave at any moment and not have a thing to pack. Anyone could sit down behind the carved mahogany desk and pick up where he'd left off. Sadness for him edged out her earlier disappointment. He had one foot in, one foot out and wasn't likely to keep either in San Rey.

"Knock it off."

She started at his voice. "What?"

"I haven't had enough coffee yet to deal with whatever you were just thinking about."

"What does your tattoo mean?"

His surprise at her question quickly morphed into annoyance. "That's it. I'm firing Jessica's ass as soon as she gets it back here."

"You could just lock your door."

"If there was a lock on it." He leaned back, the creak of his chair echoing off the nearly bare walls. He watched her with tired eyes that missed nothing. "It's the Chinese word for protector. I celebrated my graduation from the police academy more than I should have and woke up with it the next morning."

"You just have the one?"

His lazy, half smile lit small fires she struggled to bank. "Maybe someday you can answer that question for yourself."

She opened her mouth to respond, but was cut off by Elmer's entrance.

Mabel came in on his heels, bustling efficiency. "Everything's all taken care of," she said. "Chris Farnsworth is now fully clothed, Pax is on his way out to Ned's, and Jessica is working on the filing. I had a chat with her. Not to worry, she'll take the time off her lunch. Is there anything you need, Sheriff?"

"Locks," Graham said under his breath, then spoke loud enough for Mabel to hear. "No interruptions until we're done here."

"You got it, Sheriff Doran." Mabel closed the door after her.

"You'd better not have started without me," Elmer said, dropping into the chair next to Erin with a grunt.

"Wouldn't think of it." Graham pressed a button on his recorder and stated the salient information for what he called the Lasiter case. "You don't have any objections to this interview being recorded, do you?" Graham asked Erin.

She shook her head.

"I need your answer audible for the recording."

"Oh. No. I don't have any objections."

. . .

GRAHAM TOOK her through the events of the day before, watching carefully for signs he was pushing her too hard. She held up. The pride he felt in that both pleased and annoyed him. He found himself focusing too often on her lips and the way they shaped words. He imagined too vividly that mouth whispering against his skin and crying out his name. Her lips pressed flat, smashing through his daydream. He realized she was waiting for him to speak.

He gulped cold coffee and cleared his throat. "Did you ever have any dealings with Deidre Lasiter?"

"Enough to say hi now and then when she lived in town. We weren't friends or anything, if that's what you're asking."

"Did you know any of her friends?"

"A few. We didn't travel in the same circle."

"Give me some names."

"Janet Weidlin, Beatrice Farnsworth, and Susie Philpot. We have... had the same hair stylist down at the Clippity-Do-Da. Candy Dougherty."

"I can arrange for you to talk to my granddaughter, Beatrice," Elmer said. "In my presence, of course."

Graham looked up from his notes. "Of course. Thanks, Elmer." Great. He looked forward to interviewing the who's who of his high school dating years — the girl he'd had a serious hard-on for, but never dated; the girl who'd had a crush on him; and the girl he'd ended up dating for nearly two years, in that order. He couldn't decide which he dreaded most. "What about Greg?" he asked Erin. "Know anything about his friends? Were he and Deidre friends with any other couples?"

Her brow creased, in confusion or censure? If he'd stayed in San Rey he'd likely know the answer to his own question, would likely *be* one of the guys Greg hung out with. The regret of that realization made him feel guilty and sad for cutting off all ties to anything or anyone San Rey, other than his immediate family. He hadn't expected to feel this way. During his time in L.A. there was no nostalgia, no looking back. There was nothing he missed or looked forward to whenever he came back for a visit. Did Erin see the total obliteration of his past as a criticism of him as a person?

"As far as I know," Erin started, "Greg hung out with the same guys since high school. Susie or Beatrice would probably know more."

"Okay. Thanks. That's it." Graham turned the recorder off. He had more to ask, but none of it was relevant to the case.

"I can leave?"

"I might have a couple of follow up questions, but for now, yeah, you can leave."

Erin gathered up her coat and bag. She paused at the door. "That wasn't as bad as I thought it would be. Thanks for that. You'll let me know about funeral arrangements?"

"I will." He waited for her to leave, then settled back into his chair.

"She's a looker like her Aunt Cerie was. Still is," Elmer amended. "Do you suppose it's true?"

"What?"

"Whatever gene it is that gives all them Decembers their woo-woo powers skipped her generation?"

"I wouldn't know," Graham hedged, annoyed. He'd heard this talk behind hands all his life. Hearing it now, about Erin, with everything she'd shared with him, pissed him off. She was right. He didn't know the first thing about what her life had been like growing up here. The whispers and judgmental looks, being painted with the same brush no matter what you did or didn't do. He didn't know how she stood it, why she stayed and put up with it.

"Probably for the best. Not many young men'd want their minds read. Not many old men either." Elmer gave the door Erin had left through a thoughtful look. "Then again, there aren't many women with a caboose like hers, is there?"

Graham's irritation ratcheted up a notch, but there was no denying the truth of Erin's attractiveness. "No. There's not."

Elmer's laugh creaked out as he left. "Good for you, sonny. Good for you."

Graham shook his head, remembering just how fine the ass in question had felt in his hands last night. He hadn't planned to kiss her. Hadn't planned to back her up against that tree. Hadn't planned the way his body had reacted to hers or hers to his. He didn't regret it either. It was probably for the best that she'd sent him home instead of inviting him in. He didn't want or need the complications that would have caused. She was dating someone else and he wasn't looking for another reason to stay in San Rey. The sooner he got through this case, the sooner he could figure another way out of this town.

He pressed the play button. Erin's voice filled the room, surrounding him. With her scent still lingering, he closed his eyes, allowing the sensation of her to press in at him, penetrating every pore until he could almost feel her. Almost recreate what it had been like to have her near.

Someone cleared his throat, jolting Graham back to reality. He switched off the recording. Mayor Ted Bhare more than filled the doorway with a good portion of him spilling into the room uninvited. *What the hell does he want?*

"Got a moment, Graham?"

Graham set aside the recorder and his notes and motioned the man in. "What can I do for you, Mayor?"

"Call me Teddy. We're all friends here, right?" Teddy lumbered into the room and wedged himself into a chair. He wheezed and shifted, finally settling into his seat like a great nesting bullfrog. "The fine citizens of San Rey are concerned about recent—" Teddy moved the next word around in his mouth before finally spitting it out, "—*incidents*. I've come for your report. Give me something I can take back to my people."

"Your people." *What fresh bullshit was this?*

"The citizenry are understandably concerned. Murder and mayhem have come to San Rey. Their way of life has been suddenly and inexplicably—" He did some more word chewing. "—*challenged*. They're looking for answers. We're all looking for answers and you're the man holding them."

Graham folded his arms and leaned back in his chair. He'd had limited experience with politicians, but enough to know they only slithered out from under their rocks when they wanted something or were plotting reelection.

"We're working leads and gathering evidence."

Teddy waved a meaty hand. "Come now, Graham. We're friends. You can give me more than that."

"I really can't. None of the lab work is back. There are no autopsy reports yet. I haven't even gotten a chance to do all the interviews I need to. Any information I give you now wouldn't do you or the citizenry any good. All we have are two victims and a lot of questions."

"Your impressions, then."

"My impressions are that I can't comment on a case that hasn't been fully investigated."

Teddy's jaw worked. "*Semantics*."

"It would be irresponsible of us both to give the fine citizens of San Rey inaccurate or incomplete information. You're just going to have to tell them that we're working every possible lead."

"I understand your position. I really do. So we'll just keep this between you and me." Teddy winked with the effort most people put into a push up.

Except with a politician, nothing was likely to stay where it didn't do him the most good. Why was Teddy pushing so hard? What did he want with the information? What was he going to do with it? Could he somehow be involved in what happened at the Lasiters' house? Great. He was going to have to add the mayor to his list of possible suspects, which was pathetically short.

"I'll tell you what. As soon as I have something, you'll be the first to know." Graham stood. "I give you my word."

Teddy heaved himself to his feet, his face mottled red with the effort as he faced Graham across the desk. "I respect your family's fine...*tradition*. Your father was a sheriff who knew his job. I expect he's got a few ropes he still needs to show you." Teddy's marbled gaze rolled about the room, over the portraits of Graham's ancestors, coming to rest on the badge clipped to Graham's shirt pocket. "I expect you'll learn the way of things...*yet*."

As Teddy lurched toward the door Graham felt the eyes of his forefathers watching, judging. He'd only been on the job a couple weeks and had already made an enemy of the mayor. Damned small town with its small minds and small town politics.

He dug his fingernails into the underside of the polished walnut desk. The ever-present urge to get the hell out rose up inside him, lodging hard and suffocating in his chest. He shouldn't have come back to San Rey. Shouldn't have let his father guilt him in to taking over as sheriff.

And he sure as hell should never have touched Erin December.

8

Rumors and speculation catapulted what had happened at the Lasiter house into the story of the century in San Rey, with Erin at the center of it all. People who hadn't spoken to her in weeks suddenly sought her out, wanting the gory details, when they weren't pointing at her and whispering about her behind their hands with their friends. She was now notorious for an entirely different reason.

She wouldn't have risked an outing to the hair salon unless she was desperate. As usual for a Saturday, the Clippity-Do-Da was packed. Erin tried to keep to herself and ignore the furtive looks from the other ladies having their hair done. So when the blatant stares turned away from her and toward the door, Erin couldn't help but turn to see what or who had snagged their attention.

Graham.

He looked haggard and drawn. She hadn't seen him since the morning she gave her statement, but she could tell the case was wearing on him. Her own dark circled eyes and pale complexion gave away the fact that she wasn't sleeping well either. She had to admit that she'd missed the sight of him. The usual feminine salon chatter shrank to appreciative whispers as the door whooshed closed behind him.

He spoke to the receptionist who immediately approached Erin's hairstylist to let her know that Graham was there to see her. Erin slid deeper into her seat. Graham recognized her anyway with a twitch of a smile. Ignoring the stares and murmurs of the lady patrons, he settled onto the waiting area couch with a People magazine, giving it all of his attention.

Leaning close to Erin's foiled head, Candy whispered, "He's here to talk to me about Deidre and Greg. I still can't believe they're gone."

"Me either," Erin responded. Candy was one of the few people who hadn't pumped her for information about the murder/suicide.

"I just don't get it. How could Greg have killed her? *Why?* Their divorce was amicable. I know he'd recently lost his job and was losing his house. It's just so…"

"Horrible."

Candy met Erin's gaze in the mirror. "Yeah. I guess you'd know about that. Did Greg say anything? Tell you why he did it?"

And there it was. The question she'd been asked a million times. Erin dropped her voice so no one would overhear. "He didn't kill her."

"He said that?"

Erin nodded.

Candy shook her head. "And you believed him? Why?"

How to answer? Candy had been more of a friend to her than anyone, but it wasn't as though Erin could tell her about the vision of Deidre opening the door to her killer or seeing the murder through the killer's eyes. There were some details she couldn't bring herself to think about, let alone talk about. Except with Graham.

"I just do," Erin finally answered.

"I'm going to miss her. Deidre could be...difficult sometimes, but she didn't deserve to die."

"No. She didn't."

Candy continued to work on Erin's hair, but she didn't ask any more questions. Thankfully she changed topics to talk about something funny her dog had done. Erin was grateful she didn't press for more.

Candy painted color onto the last foil and folded it up. "Come on. Let's put you under the dryer."

Erin followed Candy to the bank of dryers at the back of the salon where a couple of other clients sat getting pink cheeked. Candy fiddled with the knobs, then lowered the hood over Erin's head. Erin had a perfect view of the front of the salon. She watched Candy stroll up to Graham with a little extra swing in her skin-tight jeans. She flipped her purple streaked hair and laughed as Graham rose from the couch and tossed the magazine aside. They went outside and sat at the café table in front of the window.

"They'd make a nice couple," the woman next to Erin said with a sigh to her friend on her other side. "We need a sheriff who's settled."

"He should be spending more time controlling crime than flirting with girls," the friend harrumphed. "It's gotten so I won't go out at night."

"Me either. Did you hear how Doreen got her purse snatched right on Main Street?"

Erin tuned out the complaining women, too caught up in the scene at the front of the salon. Candy leaned an elbow on the table, her chin in her hand. Every now and then she'd reach over and touch Graham's arm as he wrote in his notebook. At one point he smiled at something Candy said. His real smile, the one he'd teased Erin with. Erin tried not to be jealous of Candy and had almost convinced herself she wasn't when Graham leaned closer to Candy. He said something, then winked, eliciting a lingering stroke on his arm from Candy. Was he flirting with Candy? Erin knew she didn't have the right to be mad at how close Graham and Candy were, but *son of a bitch*. It wasn't that long ago that Graham was paying Erin that kind of attention.

The tone of the conversation outside seemed to change. Graham and Candy's body language shifted, going from teasing to serious. They moved a little closer across the table, mirroring each other's poses. Candy pulled the pen out of Graham's grasp, reached for his other hand, and wrote something on his palm. She tapped the end of the pen against her lips, then handed it back to him. They rose from the table as Erin's dryer clicked off. Candy gave Graham a hug and waved goodbye to him, then stood a few minutes more, watching him walk away. She turned to come back in with little a shiver.

Candy couldn't seem to suppress her grin as she made her way to Erin. She dipped her head shyly when one of her coworkers teased her about Graham, but didn't comment.

"Let me check to see if you're done," Candy said, lifting the dryer hood and opening one of the foils on Erin's head. "You're good. Let's get you shampooed."

Erin followed Candy to the shampoo area, then lay back in the chair with her head in the shampoo bowl. The scent of permanent wave solution and bleach was sharper here, stinging Erin's nose as Candy pulled the foils from her hair and began rinsing the color out.

"You know there's just something about a man in uniform," Candy said with a sigh. "Or maybe there's just something about Graham Doran."

Erin couldn't help the little arrow of jealousy that had worked its way into her chest and sprung open into claws that wouldn't let go. "So what exactly did he want to know?"

"He asked me a bunch of questions about Deidre. Who she was seeing and when was the last time I saw her. Stuff like that."

"I guess as her hairstylist you'd know what was going on with her better than most."

"You'd think, but Deidre'd been kinda secretive lately. She didn't talk too much about what was going on the last few times I saw her. Although I got the feeling something big was about to happen. I didn't think it would be her dying though." Candy trailed off, a sad frown digging between her brows.

"Who could've known?"

"It still doesn't feel real."

"No. It doesn't. What do you suppose that big thing was?"

"I don't know for sure. Like I told Graham, she seemed really happy, but I don't think it was about the divorce. I think she might've been seeing someone new. The last time she was in she asked for a new style." Candy wrapped Erin's hair in a towel and helped her sit up. "Come on back to the chair. Are we cutting your hair today or are you still growing it out?"

"Growing it out," Erin said as she sat in the styling chair. "Keith likes my hair long." One more way in which she was trying with him. Always trying.

Candy suddenly gave combing out Erin's hair more attention than it required. "You know I had to tell Graham everything I know, right?"

There was something in Candy's expression that gave Erin an uneasy feeling. "Yeah."

"I don't spread rumors. What people tell me while they're in my chair stays with me. But I had to tell Graham. He's the police."

That uneasy feeling deepened, morphing into dread. "Had to tell him what exactly?" Erin said slowly, wanting and yet not wanting to know.

Candy cast a watchful eye around them, then whispered, "About Keith and Deidre."

Erin caught Candy's gaze in the mirror. "What about Keith and Deidre?"

"Oh, God." Candy put a hand to her chest. "You don't know. I'm sorry. I shouldn't have said anything." Candy abruptly grabbed the hair dryer and switched it on.

Erin caught Candy's wrist, stilling her. "What, Candy? Just tell me."

Candy bit her lip as though deciding something, then she turned the dryer off and leaned close. "Keith and Deidre were a couple for a while right before and maybe a little after you and he started going out. I really thought you knew. But this doesn't have to change anything between you and Keith. You're so great together and I can see how much you like him and he likes you."

But it did change things. The vision Erin had of Keith and his mother in that kitchen now had context. Keith had been seeing Deidre and might have gotten her pregnant while he and Erin had been dating. Could Keith be responsible for Deidre's death? Was that why he'd been so solicitous toward Erin and had shown up at the police station—out of guilt? Who else knew about his and Deidre's relationship? Did Greg know?

Erin looked up into her hairstylist's anxious face and felt as though she was expected to make Candy feel better about her revelation. But all she could do was smile weakly and wonder if what she and Keith had shared was real or was their relationship nothing more than smoke and mirrors, the perfect distraction from his affair with Deidre?

"It's okay," Erin finally managed with a one-shoulder shrug that was more of a jerk. "No biggie. Don't worry about it."

"Oh, I'm so relieved. I don't want to cause any trouble between the two of you."

"No. No trouble. No trouble at all."

Candy switched the dryer back on and began blow-drying Erin's hair, chatting amiably about nothing in particular. Erin nodded and responded appropriately, but all the while her mind spun.

Keith and Deidre. If Keith was upset over Deidre's death, he didn't show it. Had Keith's insistence on taking things to the next level with Erin been a way to ease his guilt over his relationship with Deidre? Or was it to avert attention away from his and Deidre's relationship after her death? That would explain why he suddenly wanted to get out of town for a while.

Deidre hadn't been expecting the man who'd killed her—a married man. At least that's the impression Erin had gotten from her vision of Deidre and the killer. What if she'd read the vision wrong? The killer was definitely someone who enjoyed his stature in the community. His thoughts about that had been very clear. As Erin had explained to Graham, Keith was well respected and admired in San Rey. He'd earned a repu-tation of charity and goodness. Getting a married woman pregnant would certainly affect his standing in the community.

Would Keith have killed Deidre to protect his good name? Was Keith the father of Deidre's baby? Could her pregnancy have played a part in what happened to her?

Erin jumped when Candy turned off the hairdryer. She'd been so absorbed in her thoughts she hadn't paid any attention and now Candy was frowning at her.

"You're upset," Candy said. "I shouldn't have told you."

"No, really. I'm okay. I was just thinking about work," Erin lied.

Candy whisked the color cape off of Erin and rearranged Erin's hair over her shoulders. "How do you like your new highlights?"

"They're great. Just what I wanted. Thank you."

"I should be done around seven. Do you want to go for a drink or something tonight?"

Erin got up slowly, tamping down the urge to flee. Her thoughts had stirred up emotions she had no defense against. She picked up her purse and turned to her friend. "Thanks, but I have plans tonight."

"With Keith?"

"Yes."

Candy put a hand on Erin's arm. "Please don't let what I said ruin your night with him."

How could it not? "I won't. Thanks again for my hair."

Erin backed away, the rising need to escape making her feel shaky and weak. She paid for her hair and bolted, hitting the sidewalk at a brisk pace. She hardly registered the stares and whispers of the townsfolk as she passed. She turned right on Wicker Street and followed it up and around as it narrowed and the sidewalk gave way to a dirt path. The hard packed earth floated around her ankles as she trudged further up to where expensive homes with ocean views gave way to modest bungalows tucked into the side of the hill, shut off from the impressive vistas.

She spotted the police cruiser parked out front of her small house and slowed her pace, trying to imagine why it would be there. Then she caught sight of Graham leaning against the porch railing, waiting for her. His mirrored sunglasses glinted in the afternoon sunlight, but she knew he watched her progress as she came up her steep front walk. Without a word he peeled off the pillar and followed her into the house, not needing an invitation. She knew why he'd come. He was here to ask her about Keith and Deidre.

She hung her jacket on a hook in the entryway. He did the same and trailed after her toward the kitchen. It was a short walk. These old bungalows tucked into the rolling hills above San Rey were no bigger than a two-bedroom apartment. But there was a little plot of sloping land out back where Erin had envisioned a tiered garden that had cemented her decision to buy. The garden now filled the view from the window over the sink, row upon row of flowers and herbs poured over the boxed edges of the beds. The aroma of fall flowers wafted in, scenting the whole house.

"Iced tea?" she asked, reaching into the refrigerator, stalling. She hadn't yet processed her thoughts and feelings, let alone come to the point where she could translate them for Graham.

"Sure."

She could feel him, watching, waiting as she put ice in the glasses and poured the tea. Did he think she knew about Deidre and Keith's affair? She couldn't figure out which he would think was worse—her knowing and not doing or saying anything about it or her not knowing and being cheated on by her boyfriend.

"Sweetener?" she asked, hoping to extend her hostess duties.

"No. Black is fine."

She took a breath and faced him across the small kitchen island, needing the barrier.

He reached for the glass she offered, their fingers brushing briefly. Had that simple, accidental touch affected him the way it had her? Did he feel turned inside out and backwards the way she did? She fought for some equilibrium, searching for some sense of what he was thinking in his expression.

He set his sunglasses on the counter and sipped his tea, taking in everything about her. "I like your hair."

"Thanks."

She grew warm under his watchful gaze, which lingered improperly on areas it shouldn't. Alone together, he didn't bother to hide his attraction for her. It would be so easy to show him hers. He had her so twisted up and off balance, she hardly trusted herself around him.

"Why are you here?" she asked, gripping her glass with both hands.

"The coroner confirmed that Deidre was pregnant."

She nodded.

"We won't have the DNA results back for a few

more weeks, maybe months, depending on how back-logged the lab is."

"You're testing the fetus against Greg's DNA?"

"Yeah."

"But he's not the father."

"It's not like I can take samples from every man Deidre ever had contact with." He put the insinuation of the baby possibly being Keith's out there for her to pick up in open challenge. His expression gave away nothing as he waited for her response.

Did he think she'd known about Deidre and Keith and had lied to protect her boyfriend? It would almost be better if that were the case. At least then she wouldn't have to admit that Keith had deceived her. That he was lying to her still. That what was between her and Keith was tainted and wrong after she'd defended their relationship so vehemently.

"No. I suppose not," she said a little too defensively, her body rigid with denial.

He lowered his gaze to his glass, smoothing the condensation from the sides. That's when she noticed the phone number Candy had written on his hand. She wondered if he'd use it. "I have to follow up on every lead," he said.

"You should," she spat back.

He lifted his head, zeroing in on her. "*Every* lead."

"San Rey's a small town. What you do and don't do is big news."

"And if I'm seen talking to someone, people will assume that person has knowledge of a crime. Or was involved in one."

"People can think what they like."

"What do *you* think, Erin?"

"I think..." She took a sip of tea to buy some time.

There were too many thoughts chasing each other around in her head to pin down a coherent one. Anything she said about Keith and Deidre would splash back on her. Was Keith using their relationship to cover up his affair with Deidre and the possibility that he was the father of Deidre's baby? Going further with that train of thought: could Keith be using their relationship to throw suspicion off him for killing Deidre and his unborn child?

Erin had to choose her words carefully here. Not everyone would think she was innocent and they might even think she conspired with Keith if he turned out to be a murderer. Worse yet, Graham might think she conspired with Keith by making up the visions she saw to throw Graham off Keith's trail.

"I think it's more important to find out what actually happened than to worry about what people will assume," she answered.

And that was the truth. People could bend facts to suit their purposes, but they couldn't change them.

She puffed out a breath, her mind made up. "You *should* pursue every lead. Every last one."

"Even if that means stirring up the gossip hive?"

She looked out the window at the waning daylight. Keith would be there in about an hour to pick her up for their date. "You can give them something to talk about tomorrow, can't you?" She turned back to find him examining her intently.

They stared at each other across the island, the tension between them hard and tight. She tried to communicate with her eyes what she couldn't with her words. If he gave her this, she'd owe him.

"It can wait until tomorrow. Only for you," he added. "This one time."

If she could get the words out, she'd thank him. Tomorrow Graham would question Keith about his relationship with Deidre and Erin would have freed herself from Keith and the shadow that had hovered over their relationship. It was a relief. She finally had a reason for why she couldn't ever make things work with Keith. All along it was his fault and not a flaw that lay deep within her. He'd poisoned their relationship from the start. There was no going back from that.

"There's one other thing," Graham said. "Deidre's cell phone and keys were missing from the things we found of hers at the house. Know anything about that?"

She closed her eyes for a moment, picturing the kitchen where Deidre and Greg had died. "No," she drew out after a moment, opening her eyes. "I don't recall them."

"Have you had any more visions?"

She thought about the one she'd had of Keith and his mother. She'd asked a lot of Graham and he'd given it to her when he didn't have to. She owed him the full truth.

"I'm trying not to have any at all. But it seems as though I don't have a choice in the matter anymore." She described the vision she'd inadvertently had of Keith in his mother's kitchen, which had taken on a whole new meaning now that she knew about Keith and Deidre's affair. It wasn't easy to tell after she'd defended Keith to Graham so vehemently.

"Shit." He put a hand on her arm. "I'm sorry."

"Me too."

"Are still you having pain with the visions?"

She was grateful to him for the subject change and for not delving further into what her vision could mean. "Pain and a bright light that whites out everything. It's almost as though someone flips a switch, filling my mind with blinding white light."

"What about your aunt and father?"

"Aunt Cerie is having the most trouble," she answered. "My dad and I learned how to shut her out to keep her from reading our thoughts. She never learned to block off her mind that way so for her, the light keeps burning. She's exhausted, but can't sleep. The more she uses her ability, the more she has these episodes."

"Has she thought about seeing a doctor?"

"I've been trying to get her to go, but she's resisting. Not many people can get my aunt to do something she doesn't want to."

"I bet."

"Are there any new leads?" she asked.

"We're following a few threads. Mostly we're waiting on lab results. There was a surprise in the autopsy report though. Deidre had sex within a few hours of her death. No semen, but there was a hair sample we're testing."

"Do you think she might have had sex with her baby's father?" Keith or someone else?

"It's a strong possibility. We do know that both Deidre and Greg were shot with the gun that was found at the scene. Only Greg's fingerprints were on it though."

"The killer wore gloves. Leather. Black. They squeaked." She shuddered, reliving her vision of the killer entering the house to commit murder.

"Can you think of anything else? Any details you haven't mentioned before? Maybe something new you're just remembering?"

"No."

"Let me know if you do." Graham climbed off the barstool. "Thanks for the tea."

"Sure." She followed him to the door where he pulled on his coat.

He turned to the door, then back. "One more thing."

"What?"

"This."

He reached for her, pulling her into his arms. She went without question, wrapping her arms around him, the scent of him familiar and thrilling. His chest was warm against her cheek. He smoothed a hand over her hair. She closed her eyes, savoring the sensations that barreled through her. Somehow this embrace was more intimate than the kisses they'd shared, more dangerous. She soaked up the comfort he offered, wanting to hold onto him as long as she could.

"I'm worried about you confronting Keith."

"I'll be fine."

"I bet Deidre thought the same thing."

His words made her take a step back from him. "He

wouldn't hurt me."

"No?"

"It wasn't him I saw in my vision of Deidre's death."

"How can you be sure?"

"I just am. It wasn't him. I don't know how to explain it other than it didn't *feel* like him."

He looked like he might argue the point, then changed his mind. "Call me afterward. Let me know how it went."

"Why?"

"So I know you're okay."

"I'll be fine. You should go. The longer you stay, the more stories my neighbors will invent about why you're here."

"Call me," he insisted, reaching for the doorknob. "No matter how late."

"That's not a good idea." Furthering this whatever it was between them would only make her life more complicated. But oh, how she wished she were brave enough to accept the unspoken challenge in his eyes.

He must've seen something in her face that belied her words. "Call me and we're even."

"Fine."

The edges of his mouth kicked up into the smile she had a hard time looking away from. "It's just a check-in call, Erin. Not a hook-up call."

"That's not... I didn't think..."

He opened the door, laughing as he went down her walk to his car. *Dang that man.*

But she was smiling as she closed the door after him.

"You're not dressed," Keith said when Erin opened the door to him. "Not that you don't look great." He gave her his charming smile, the one he reserved for difficult customers at the store.

"Come in." Erin gestured him inside, her pulse kicking out a ragged beat, her mouth dry. He looked different. Or maybe it was her seeing him through different eyes.

"Aren't you feeling well?" He stepped across the threshold and followed her into the living room. "I guess we can stay in. I'll have to make a quick call to cancel our reservation though."

"Sit down, Keith."

"When your girlfriend tells you to sit down with that look on her face, it can't be good." He sat on the sofa, his chuckle forced and off. "Next you're going to tell me we need to talk."

"We do."

"What's this about? I thought things were going great."

She eased into the chair opposite him. "They were."

"*Were...* Look, I don't have to stay over tonight. If you're not ready—"

"It's not about that."

"Then what's going on? You're making me nervous here."

"I need to ask you something."

"Oh, I get it." He relaxed back, laughing a little, his cheeks pinkening. "We should have talked about this sooner. It's nothing to be embarrassed about."

She blinked at him, thrown off. "It's not?"

"You're entitled to know about my past. I'd ask about yours, but a guy wants to imagine there was no one before him."

"*My* past?"

"I want you to know I'm, uh...clean. And I brought protection. That's the man's duty, right?"

"No, Keith." Oh, god. This conversation was quickly spinning out of her control. "That's not it."

"I should probably ask if you're on, ah...birth control."

"I am, but that's not what I wanted to talk with you about."

He tilted his head to one side, studying her as though she was the lock to the store safe and he'd forgotten the combination.

She decided she'd better just spit it out. "I know you had an affair with Deidre Lasiter."

He jerked as though she'd slapped him. "I—"

"Were you the father of her baby?"

He surged to his feet, his fists flexing and unflexing. "Where'd you hear this?"

She stood too, needing to stay on even ground with him. There was something in his tone she didn't trust. "Does it matter?"

"Hell yes, it matters."

"Is it true?"

He paced away then back, his face flushed, his jaw rigid. She'd never seen this side of him. He was always so damn placid. She'd taken that calmness at face value, never imagining that it might be nothing more than a cover.

"Tell me where you heard this," he demanded.

"Why aren't you answering my question?" But she knew why.

He gripped her by the arms. Hard. "Who told you?"

She tried to break out of his hold, but he only dug his fingers in deeper, pulling her up against him. For the first time she was afraid of him. Gone was the amiable do-gooder she'd considered giving herself to. In his place was a desperate man. His panic was contagious, flowing from him into her. Her heart stuttered in her chest, her fight or flight instinct kicking in.

He gave her a shake, making her head bobble back and forth. "Who was it?"

"The sheriff," she blurted out to protect Candy and possibly herself.

Releasing her, he stumbled back and scrubbed his hands over his face. "Shit." It was the second time she'd ever heard him swear. Both in the last ten minutes. He headed for the door. "I have to go."

"Keith?"

"What?" Impatience made his answer a curse.

She swallowed a sob. "I don't want to see you anymore."

He threw open the door, causing it to bang against the wall and slam closed behind him. Her watery knees gave out and she sank down, missing the chair and hitting the floor instead. Pain shot through her. Tears stinging the backs of her eyes, she covered her face with shaking hands. She let out a breath when she heard his car start and peel away from the curb. Until tonight she'd never considered Keith could be violent. She rubbed her arms where his fingers had dug into her flesh.

For a moment she'd thought he was going strike her. Telling him Graham was the one who'd told her about Deidre might not have been the smartest thing to do. But it was the only thing she could think of at the time. And it had worked. She'd seen the fear in Keith's eyes. Her lie may have been the one thing that had saved her from Deidre's fate. She shuddered, remembering Deidre's body lying on the floor, blood pooled around her.

And then the vision struck, knocking her to the floor and flinging her out of her living room, into a darkened hotel room. Deidre laid in the bed, nude, the sheet barely covering her, exposing both her breasts and one leg. Dust motes danced in the thin beams of light that eeked through the threadbare drapes. Next to her, the large shape of a man rolled toward her, his hairy legs hanging off the end of the bed. He reached for Deidre, palming her large breast. His face shadowed, the man moved over Deidre, parting her thighs. One of his hands disappeared beneath the sheet.

Deidre shifted, raising her arms over her head and arching her back. She made a purring sound, widening her legs. The man lowered his dark head to her breast. Writhing beneath him, Deidre clutched his head to her.

"Oh, God," Deidre panted.

Erin clapped her hands over her ears and turned her head. She didn't want to see or hear this. Focusing her thoughts, she struggled to get out of the vision, but the rawness from Keith's visit made it difficult to concentrate. She fixed her gaze on a red and blue sign she could just make out through the curtains. The shape of the letters triggered a familiar memory she tried to grab a hold of. As the grunts and slaps of flesh grew louder she jammed her fingers in her ears and squeezed her eyes closed, shutting off those senses entirely.

The pain hit, stealing her breath. White-hot light filled her head. The last thing she remembered was Deidre screaming out Keith's name.

GRAHAM SAT AT HIS PARENTS' dining table with his dad, waiting for his mom to bring in dinner. She'd insisted on making Sunday dinner for the family. Today had been one of her 'good days' so no one told her it was

Saturday or that Graham's brother Adam wasn't away at camp, but overseas on military assignment. His mother's spiral into dementia had taken a toll on the whole family, especially Ham, and the stress from it had probably contributed to his heart condition.

At the head of the table, Ham sipped a glass of the Cabernet Graham had brought to go with the pot roast his mother was making. Sweat dotted Ham's upper lip and despite the chill breeze wafting in from the open window, his face was flushed. He'd already barked at Graham for asking if he was okay, so Graham kept his worried glances to a minimum.

"How's the case going?" Ham asked. "Any new leads?"

"A few, but nothing conclusive."

"Save the party line for the mayor and city council."

The last thing Graham wanted to do was cause his father any more distress. He weighed the options and decided his dad would be more upset about being treated as an invalid than he would by the details of the case. So he updated him on the information he'd gathered so far.

"It could take weeks or months for the lab to cough up the DNA results," Graham said. "Meanwhile the District Attorney is after us to come up with some kind of evidence that would point to it being something other than the murder/suicide it appears to be. So far we have zilch."

"Have you considered that it might be just as it appears? If it walks like a duck and quacks like a duck..."

"I have, but my gut tells me it's not."

Ham took another sip of wine. "Speaking of the mayor, he paid me a visit this morning."

Graham sat up a little straighter in his chair. "What did he want?" But he already knew and it pissed him off.

"He's concerned. And so am I."

"Don't start."

"Why don't you tell me what you've able to piece together about the victims?"

"So you can report back to the mayor?"

Ham narrowed his gaze. "I don't report to him or anyone."

"You used to."

"Not anymore."

Graham weighed what to divulge and what to share that would placate his father, while maintaining the integrity of the case.

"We know that Deidre was having an affair with a local man. He might have been the father of her baby. From the timeline we've been able to put together, she got pregnant after she and Greg split up. But that doesn't necessarily mean Greg wasn't the father. They could have had a brief reconciliation. Won't know for sure until the DNA results come back."

"She was pregnant?"

Graham nodded.

Ham finished off his glass of wine in two gulps. "And the husband?"

"Greg's been tougher to pin down. He seems to have kept to himself a lot in the months since Deidre left him and he lost his job. His house was foreclosed on and as far as we can tell, he had made plans to move to Arizona. He rented an apartment and found a new job with his cousin's company near Phoenix. Everything I've discovered about him says he was moving on. He was meeting Deidre to sign the final divorce papers and had an appointment with the company that had bought his house to hand over his keys." Graham shrugged. "None of that suggests to me that he was planning to kill Deidre, then himself."

"Desperate people do desperate things."

"From everything I could gather about him before the day of the shooting, Greg wasn't desperate. He was planning a new life." And that life had been stolen from him.

"Maybe Greg didn't plan to kill his wife," Ham said conversationally. "Maybe it was a spur of the moment kind of thing."

"The gun was unregistered. Who just happens to bring an unregistered weapon to sign divorce papers and hand over the keys to their house?" Graham shook his head. "I don't buy it."

"How local was the man she was having an affair with?"

"Very."

"You know who it was?"

"Keith Collins."

Ham wiped his upper lip with a handkerchief. "What'd he have to say when you talked to him?"

"That's number one on my to-do list tomorrow. Should I go check on Mom?"

"She's fine," Ham said. "The mayor's also concerned that the additional patrols aren't having the desired results."

"The mayor can go to h—"

Ham pointed a shaky finger at his son. "Not in my house."

"We're doing the best we can with what we've got."

"Are you?"

Graham's mother, Catherine, came into the dining room, balancing a large platter in her thin arms. Her frailty frightened Graham in a way Ham's heart problem didn't. She was wasting away, both mentally and physically. Graham leapt up to take the platter from her and set it on the table.

"Wait," Catherine said. "I need to put something down first. A what's-it-called." She put a hand to her forehead. "What is it called?" She spun on her heals and headed back to the kitchen.

Left holding the platter, Graham looked to his father. Ham shrugged.

Ham cleared his throat, a sure sign he was settling in for a lecture. "Dorans have been sheriffs in San Rey for—"

"I know, Pop."

"Here it is." Catherine came in waving a carved wooden disc. She put it on the table. "Okay, now you can set it down. Peas! I made peas." She dashed out of the room again.

"I don't think you do," Ham said. "And neither does the mayor."

Graham could feel the anger crawling up his throat.

He started to lower the platter, then pulled it back up again. "Where did you get that wood thing?" he asked Ham.

"The trivet? I made it in that wood working club the doctor made me join to lower my stress. It was either that or yoga." Ham jabbed his finger at Graham. "Don't change the subject."

"What's it made of?"

"Some exotic wood called Purple Heart. What's all the interest?"

Graham set the platter down. "I found some purple sawdust in the kitchen at the Lasiter house. It was the same color as this Purple Heart wood. Who else is in this woodworking club?"

"Let me see." Ham settled back in his chair and dabbed at his forehead. "Ray Fine of Fine's Hardware teaches the class. Then there's Chris and Nick Farnsworth, Bill Nater, Mayer Behre, Donald December, Keith Collins, and Greg Lasiter."

"So nearly half the town, including one of my victims. Damn. I was hoping it would've been the piece of evidence that blew open the case."

"I told you to watch your mouth in my house."

"Sorry, Pop."

Catherine came in with a cake and stopped abruptly, staring down at the pot roast with a frown. Her gaze bounced back and forth between the cake and pot roast. "I made a carrot cake," she finally said, her brows drawn together.

Graham stood and took the plate from her. "Come and sit down, Mom." He helped her into her chair and poured her a glass of wine. "Let me know what you think of the wine I brought. I'll go and grab the peas for you."

She blinked up at him. "Peas? I always make carrots and potatoes with a roast. You know that."

"Oh, good. I don't like peas." Graham patted his mother's thin shoulder and escaped into the kitchen.

He found the oven still on so he switched it off. No carrots and potatoes inside. He lifted the lid off the steaming pot on the stove and found nothing but boiling water. After a quick riffle through the freezer he found some lima beans, so he dumped them in the water to cook. The evidence of his mother's illness was everywhere in the kitchen. A misplaced item here, a task half done there. Little things that added up, forcing Graham to confront the fact that his mother was slipping away from him one oven mitt in the refrigerator at a time.

He stirred the lima beans, remembering the time when his mom had taught him to make grilled cheese sandwiches on this very stove. She'd been patient and had ignored his teenage protest that he didn't need to learn how to cook when there was fast food.

"Fast food is expensive," she'd said. "And I want to know my boys are going to eat more than cheap ramen and microwaved dinners."

Graham had made countless grilled cheese sandwiches since then and every time he'd mentally thanked his mother's determination. To see her now so unsure of herself, so scattered, shook him. He stared down into the pan, watching the water bubble around the beans, knowing he'd been away from home too long. He wanted to leave again, at the same time he knew he couldn't. The thought of his father, shrunken and gray looking as he was tonight, standing on the porch with his mother, her brow pinched in confusion, waving goodbye as Graham drove away... hell.

Damn it to all hell.

Switching off the burner, he knew he couldn't leave. Not like this. Not with both his parents the way they were. He bent over, leaning on the counter for support. Just the thought of staying in this town twisted his gut into knots. He saw himself eating lunch at the Do or Dine every Friday, cracking jokes with the old timers who hung out at Fine's Hardware, and tipping his hat to the Ladies Auxiliary as he passed the VFW hall the same as his father had done and his father before him and so on. Having to hear, practically every day, how he didn't live up to the Doran legacy. Everything he'd gone off to Los Angeles to avoid. And then he'd screwed things up there.

Maybe he could get them a live-in nurse. As soon as he had the thought, he knew his pop would never go for it. Ham would see through it for the cop out it was and would never accept the help. He'd insist they could take care of themselves. Damn, Adam, for leaving him to handle all this by himself.

"Graham?" His mother padded into the kitchen. "Come and eat. Dinner's getting cold."

"Sure, Mom. Just grabbing the lima beans."

"Lima beans?" She glanced around the kitchen as though she was looking for something.

"Thanks for making them for me instead of potatoes and carrots. You know how much I love lima beans."

She tilted her head and her expression cleared as she took the foothold he offered her. "Anything for you, honey."

He followed his mother out of the kitchen, noticing how stooped she'd become, how thin her hair was, and how she'd forgotten to do the buttons of her blouse at the nape. Ham straightened in his seat and swiped the handkerchief across his forehead as they re-entered the dining room, pretending he hadn't been hunched over in pain.

Graham helped his mother into her chair and took his seat. She reached her hand out to Graham across the table. It had been so long since Graham had said grace before eating that it took him a moment to react. Her hand was too small and fragile in his, like a bird wing made of glass. He averted his gaze, trying to avoid how thin her skin was, how the veins stood too proud, blue streaks running through age spots, and how her wedding ring no longer fit, the setting sliding off center.

On his other side he took Ham's hand. Growing up, he'd measured his own hands against his father's so often he couldn't deny the changes that were there, too, how old and shaky Ham had become. He bowed his head, not in prayer, but in acknowledgment that the two people he'd relied on all his life now depended on him. Whether they realized it or not. Whether he wanted the responsibility or not.

He listened to Ham recite the prayer he'd said every

night of Graham's childhood. With his eyes closed, Graham could hear the strain in his father's voice, the boom of it dampened by illness and age. Graham prayed for the first time in years, asking for more time with his parents and the strength to stay and endure it.

"Amen," Ham finished and pulled his hand from Graham's at the same moment his mother did.

Graham hesitated before dragging his hands into his lap. The cold emptiness left behind at their withdrawal echoed in every corner of his mind and body.

"Amen," Graham repeated, sending his prayer off with a measure of guilt.

"You should've invited Susie for dinner," Catherine said to Graham.

Ham paused in the act of slicing the roast to give Graham a meaningful stare. She was talking about Susie Philpot, his high school girlfriend, Graham suddenly realized.

Graham grabbed the spoon for the lima beans and shoveled some onto his plate, avoiding his mother's gaze. "She has a report due tomorrow."

"That's too bad. I was hoping we could coordinate your outfits for prom... or is it winter formal?"

"The one that's held in the fall," Ham interrupted. "Please pass the lima beans, Cate."

"Lima beans?"

"I got it, Mom." Graham handed the pan to Ham, and Catherine, like a train jumping tracks, launched into a story about picking pumpkins in the fall with her sisters when she was a child.

Jiggling his leg like a piston, Graham kept his head

down and his mouth full. It was all too much. He'd avoided his parent's reality, but it had chased him down, pinning him beneath its weight. He could almost hear the crashing surf of the bluffs, luring him like a lover, the need to escape rising with every forkful of food. He wished his phone would ring.

Then he remembered that Erin should've called him.

Something was wrong. He didn't know how he knew, he just did. He dropped his fork with a clatter, startling a gasp of reproach out of his mother, and pulled his phone from his pocket. Nothing.

"Duty calls?" Ham asked, a note of reprimand in his voice.

"What? Yeah." Graham jammed his phone in his pocket and took the excuse his father handed him. "Gotta run." He leapt up and came around the table to kiss his mother on the cheek. "Thanks for dinner, Mom. It was delicious."

"Where are you going?" she asked. "I made a cake."

Graham inched toward the door. "Save me a piece?"

Ham patted his wife's hand. "Let the boy go. He's anxious to see his girl." Ham gave his wife's hand a squeeze that Graham felt deep in his chest. "I remember being just as eager to see my girl."

"Oh, Ham."

"Why don't we take our cake upstairs?" He heard his dad whisper suggestively to his mom.

Graham was out the door before his mother answered. His parents' relationship both embarrassed him and made him proud. Sometimes late at night he'd wonder if he'd ever have what they have. If he'd ever settle down and have kids. If he'd ever want his son to be a cop just like him.

With a chirp of tires, he pulled away from his parents' house. As he wound his way through the darkened streets of San Rey, his thoughts went to Erin and why she hadn't called. He pulled out his phone and dialed her number. It went straight to voicemail. He tossed his phone into the cup holder and pressed harder on the gas pedal, careening around the corner where Fine's Hardware stood. He passed the Clippity-Do-Da and turned onto the street that would take him to Erin's house.

Her house was dark, but her car was parked in the drive. That didn't mean anything. She could have walked into town or, he thought—with more animosity than he should have—she could've decided to overlook the affair between Keith and Deidre and gone out on a date with her boyfriend. He slammed his car door harder than necessary and stomped up her front steps. He knocked, then knocked again. The silence that greeted him ratcheted up the sensations he'd had when he realized she should've called. Somewhere in the distance a dog barked.

Why hadn't she called?

She should've left the porch light on. The sense that something was off fisted inside his chest, constricting his breath. He examined the door and the frame, fighting off the urge to boot the door open and charge inside. No sign of forced entry. The windows were closed, but the curtains were parted slightly. He wres-

tled with the bushes beneath the window to get a look
inside. Cupping his hands around his eyes, he peered
through the window. A light was on somewhere deeper
inside the house. Something was off. His instincts
screamed at him.

He crept around to the back of the house, passing
through a half gate into the backyard. The rich scent of
foliage and damp earth filled the air. The back of the
house was even darker than the front. He'd have to talk
to her about getting motion detecting security lights.

A noise in the bushes froze him in place. He
listened hard over the beating of his heart as he slid his
weapon from the holster and held it against his thigh.
A cat leapt onto the path in front of him. He'd raised
his arm to aim before recognition hit and he lowered
the gun back to his side again. Damn cat.

The wooden back porch steps creaked beneath his
feet as he crept toward the back door. The house was
just as still and quiet on this side. *She's in trouble.* The
thought hit him hard, knocking him down a step. He
charged toward the door and banged on it.

"Erin!"

Nothing.

He tried the knob, but it was locked. He raced
around the house to the front door. He pounded on it
with the flat of his hand.

"Erin!"

This time the knob twisted in his hand. He went in
low, gun raised. Silence. He mentally sketched the
layout of the house as he remembered it. The living
room was first, the kitchen at the back, a hall opened on

the right. He slid his feet across the hardwood, not wanting to trip over something. He thought about calling out again, but if Erin was able to hear she would have answered his earlier calls.

He came to the turn into the living room, paused, then went low around the corner. A lamp lay on its side on the floor behind the couch. The light he'd seen through the window. Yeah, definitely something wrong here. He scanned what he could see of the room in the dimness. His gaze snagged on something sticking out from behind the couch.

A hand.

He raced forward.

Erin lay sprawled on her back, her face turned toward him. A thin stream of blood oozed from her nose into the carpet.

Graham sank to his knees beside Erin, his heart galloping in his chest. He placed two fingers to her neck. Her pulse was slow, but measurable. His breath whooshed out and he gripped his knees to keep from collapsing next to her.

She was alive.

His training kicked in and he was back on his feet, gun up. Whoever had done this to her could still be in the house. He reached for his phone to call for back up, remembering too late that he'd left it in the car. He strained to listen. Nothing. Inching his way across the floor, he checked the rest of the house. Empty. Whoever had attacked her was gone.

He dropped back down beside her. "Erin." He patted her cheek. "Come on, Erin. Wake up."

She moaned, turning her face away.

"That a girl. Come on." He took her hand and rubbed it between his. "Wake up and give me shit like you always do."

"I only give you the shit you deserve," she murmured.

He grinned like the fool he was when she was near. "That's true."

"Where...?" Blinking, she looked up at him and in that moment all he wanted to do was hug her and tell her it would be okay. "What happened?" she asked.

"You tell me. Who did this to you? Please tell me it was that goofy grocer so I have a reason to punch him in the face."

"He left... I think." She struggled to sit up.

He held her shoulders down. "Stay put. I'm calling an ambulance."

"No. Don't. No one did this to me...exactly."

"What does that mean?"

"Just let me up and I'll tell you."

"What if you hit your head? You should see a doctor."

She reached a hand up to feel her scalp. "I didn't. I'm fine. Let me up."

He watched her closely as he helped her into a sitting position.

"Let me see." He gently ran his hands through her hair, feeling for any lumps. He ignored how amazing her hair felt in his hands and just how damn good it was to be near her. After a few moments, he reluctantly removed his hands and sat back on his haunches. "No bumps."

"Told you."

"Now tell me what happened." He pulled a handkerchief from his pocket—a habit drilled into him by his father—and dabbed at the blood on her face.

"I'm bleeding?"

"Yeah," he answered grimly, holding her chin in his hand to keep her still. He could feel her watching him as he gently wiped away the blood. Each red smear was like a knife through his gut. "Here." He handed her the handkerchief to finish up, trying to hide how badly his hands were suddenly shaking as he crossed his arms. She scared the shit out of him in more ways than one. He cleared his throat and watched her wipe at her nose. "Better?"

"I never get bloody noses."

He regarded her with a frown, trying to get a handle on a few minor things like what the hell had happened here? What was her emotional and physical state? And this new, perplexing awareness he associated only with her.

"What caused it?" he asked.

"I had another vision, but before I could get control of it I got broadsided."

"Broadsided."

"That's the only way I can describe it except that it was kind of like getting hit over the head with a metal folding chair."

"That's happened to you before?" he asked, his head jerking back in surprise.

"No. Of course not."

"What was the vision about?"

"Keith having sex with Deidre."

He made a face. "Eww."

"Yeah. That was my sentiment. I turned away from the...scene to look outside—"

"You can do that?" he interrupted.

"Usually. If I can focus on something else in the room, I can work my way out of it. But this time I turned to look out the window, concentrating on the hotel sign—"

"You saw what hotel they met in?"

"Yeah, something about it was familiar." She put a hand to her forehead and closed her eyes.

He settled on the floor next to her. "Describe it to me."

"Red and blue. Square. On a pole in the parking lot." She lowered her hand and opened her eyes. "There were a lot of cars going by on the street out front even though it was early in the morning."

"A highway maybe? What else was around it?"

Erin tried to concentrate on Graham's questions, but with him so close it was difficult to separate her memories from the tangle of emotions his proximity stirred up. "There was a *McDonald's* across the street, I think. Yes. Definitely a Mickey D's. The hotel sign had a number on it, like an eight or a six... *Super 6*!"

"That's good. Anything else?"

"No. I think that's it."

"Now tell me what happened between you and the cheating check-out clerk."

"Keith?"

"Is there another one?" Was that jealousy tugging his mouth down into a frown?

"Why do you want to know?"

"I'm interviewing him tomorrow."

"Can I at least get up off the floor before reliving my humiliation?"

"Sure." He helped her to her feet, which weren't as steady as she wanted them to be. "Easy. Come and sit down." He guided her to the couch, then sat down next to her. He wiggled a finger at her nose. "You got a little something…"

"I'm still bleeding?" She wiped at her nose with his handkerchief.

"No. Not blood."

"What then?" Realization dawned with burning embarrassment. "Ooohh." She covered her nose with both her hands. "I'll just go…" She eased up off the couch and headed for the bathroom, grateful to be steadier on her feet.

The sight that met her in the mirror made her gasp. She'd been talking to Graham all this time with a booger hanging out of her blood-smeared nose! She turned on the tap. While it ran to hot, she blew her nose. Why did these things always happen to her? Her cheeks burned. How horribly, awfully mortifying. First he finds her flat on her face on the floor. Then he wiped up her blood with his pristine handkerchief. And who carries a handkerchief these days anyway? And then, *then* she smeared that same handkerchief with snot.

She rinsed the poor abused cloth, scrubbing at the dried in blood. A trickle of a memory danced at the edge of her consciousness, but she couldn't quite catch a hold of it. Something from a vision maybe? She closed her eyes, trying to clear her mind and focus, but the thought slipped away. What was it? She was missing something important. She shook her head and opened her eyes. She was losing it. Maybe she really had hit her head.

After rinsing off her face, doing a minor makeup touch up, and checking her nose this way and that, Erin headed back out to the living room. Graham wasn't there. She followed faint sounds coming from the kitchen. Graham stood at the stove, his back to her, stirring something and mumbling.

"What are you doing?" she asked, her earlier embarrassment quickly morphing into surprise.

"Making you some food," he answered, without turning around.

"What? Why?"

"I'm guessing there was no dinner date so there was probably no dinner either."

She kicked the barstool back, nearly toppling it, and sat down. She propped her chin on her hand. "No. There wasn't. What are you making?"

"Chili. I found a can in your pantry." He looked at her over his shoulder. "Hungry?"

"I guess."

"Want toast?"

"No."

He went back to his stirring. "What happened with Keith?"

"I think that's the first time you've actually called him by his name and didn't find a way to make fun of him. Why the change?"

He hitched a shoulder. It was a nice shoulder and even nicer in a pair that tapered down to a V at his waist. She leaned across the counter, bringing his behind into view. A rather tight behind, snug in jeans that hugged all the right places. He chuckled and she snapped her gaze back to his in the reflection of the microwave.

"You have a nice ass," she said unapologetically. "I just noticed."

"Thanks." He winked. "So do you."

She smiled back at him. How did he do it? How did he manage to get her out of her funks when nothing and no one else usually could? "I think I'll have a glass of wine." She slid off the barstool. "Want some?"

"Sure."

"What goes with canned chili? Red or white?"

"Got any boxed wine?"

She laughed. "Heck, no. But I might have a couple bottles of Two Buck Chuck."

"Works for me."

She uncorked a bottle of red and poured two glasses. She handed one to Graham. "You're not on duty tonight?"

"No. Not really."

She pulled a couple of bowls and spoons out and set them on the countertop next to the stove. Leaning back against the counter next to him, she sipped her wine. "What does that mean 'not really'?"

"I'm the sheriff. I'm pretty much on call twenty-four-seven in a town this size."

"Sounds like you've gotten used to it."

He made a face.

"Or not." She set her glass down, deciding on a subject change. "Tell me, what happened out at Old Man Rooster's house? I heard he shot himself in the ass, trying to shoot his neighbor's dog for barking at his ugly wife."

Graham rolled his head in her direction, one corner of his mouth kicked up. He had a naughty gleam in his eye that was probably the undoing of a lot of ladies' intentions. "You really want to know?"

"I asked."

He switched off the burner and turned toward her. "What'll you give me for it?"

"Give you? You're drinking my cheap wine and are about to eat my..." He leaned toward her and she suddenly lost all thought but the memory of his lips on hers.

"Erin?" he whispered, close enough for her to catch his scent. He smelled of the ocean and something altogether new and dangerous.

"Hmm?"

"I'll tell you if you tell me what happened with Keith."

"Blackmail is beneath you."

"I always get what I want."

She lowered her gaze to his mouth. "I'm surprised you just don't take it."

"Where's the finesse in that?"

Her reply caught on a gasp as his hand grazed the back of hers. *Accidental or on purpose?*

"Tell me you broke up with him," he said.

"I did."

"How'd he take it?"

"How would you take it?"

He rested a hand on the counter next to her, leaning in. His thumb brushed the inside of her wrist. Once. Twice. "Not well."

"That makes one of you."

"Really?" He drew out the word, stretching it as thin as her resolve.

"He seemed more concerned that you knew about him and Deidre."

"What exactly did he say?" All languidness gone, Graham's gaze sharpened.

"He demanded to know who told me about their affair." Instinctively she rubbed her arms where Keith had grabbed her.

He tracked the movement. "Did he hurt you?"

"No." And that was the strangest part of all. There'd been no hurt between them. No affection either, apparently. Keith's regard was equal to hers. They'd both been forcing the relationship. She knew why she'd stayed in a relationship that never should have begun. But why did he? Was it all just a cover up for him?

"What did you tell him?"

"Just that I knew about the affair...and the baby. I asked him if he was the father."

"And?"

Flexing her fingers, she tried to smooth over the invisible imprint of Keith on her skin. The way he'd looked at her—wild, panicked—she'd never be able to blot out. "He was seriously freaked. And desperate to know who'd told me about their affair."

"Desperate?"

"How I found out was more important to him than my knowing about it." She snatched up her wine glass and stared into the ruby red liquid. "I expected more..." She made a wide gesture with her hands, sloshing her wine up the sides. "I don't know."

"Remorse?"

"Yeah." She crossed her arms and took a sip of wine. "Some remorse would've been nice."

He eased toward her. "Maybe a little groveling, too?"

"Groveling might have been a bit much."

"Probably." He captured her glass and took a sip before setting it on the counter at her hip. "But seeing him on his knees begging for your forgiveness..."

She pressed her lips together, quashing a smile.

"Ah, not too much after all," he guessed.

She playfully smacked his arm. "Stop. I'm picturing it."

Graham dropped to his knees, his hands clasped under his chin. "Please forgive me, Erin. I didn't mean to fornicate."

"Stop it." Laughing, she tried to pull him up. "Don't make fun of him."

"It's just that the freezers are so cold and she was so warm. And I'm surrounded by all those melons all day long. Please forgive me my trespasses."

She bent over, giggling, trying to tug him up off the floor. "You have to stop."

He allowed her to pull him to his feet. "I think that's the first time I've ever seen you laugh like that." He was so close, grinning down at her, his eyes creasing at the corners. "Did you know you have a dimple?" He touched her cheek with a finger. "Right there."

She wrapped her hand around his finger and brought it down between them. "Stop pointing out my flaws."

"You don't have any flaws."

Her smart-ass comeback melted on her tongue under the look in his eyes. Keith had never looked at her like that. Like a man before a buffet trying to decide which delicacy to sample first. Graham's expression boasted of lingering touches and hot open-mouthed kisses that would leave her panting for more.

"Erin?" he whispered, close enough for her to see flecks of silver in his blue eyes.

"Hmm?"

"Do you think I could kiss you?"

Her gaze dropped to his mouth. She could smell the wine on his breath as it mixed with hers. "I know you can."

"Should I though?"

"You ask stupid questions," she murmured.

And then his mouth came down on hers. He tasted of everything that was wonderful and scary. Cradling her face, he deepened the kiss. She wrapped her arms around him and moved into him, wanting so much to be closer. He broke the kiss, trailing his lips across her jaw, his beard heightening her sensitivity. Fisting his shirt, she tilted her head back for better access.

He nipped her earlobe and licked the sting. "I want you."

His declaration whispered across her senses, igniting little fires of awareness that threatened to burn out of control. She could easily lose herself in him, giving over to whatever was happening between them. She wanted to tell him how much she wanted him, too, but he was doing this thing with his mouth on her neck...

GRAHAM COULDN'T THINK. She filled up his senses, blotting out rational thought. He had his face buried in her neck, which smelled faintly Tropical, bringing with it images of beaches. And skin. Lots of bared skin under a hot sun. She moaned as he palmed her breast. Fuller than he expected. She eased onto the counter. He nestled his growing erection between her legs and she moaned again, ripping an answering groan from his throat. He wanted her naked. Right now.

"Oh, yes," she gasped, pulling up her shirt as though she'd heard his thoughts.

Slipping a hand under her top, he got his first feel of her. Soft. He kneaded the flesh at her hip and imagined gripping her from behind, thrusting into her. Hard. She pulled his head back by the hair and kissed him as she writhed against him, grinding his hard-on until he thought he'd come right there in his pants. She broke the kiss and yanked her shirt over her head. His mouth dropped open. All that creamy skin. He ran a fingertip along the top of one bra cup. She shivered and wrapped her legs around him, bringing him up against the place he most wanted to be.

He was desperate for her. The feel of her against him. Skin on skin. With her legs locked at the ankles, she unhooked her bra and shot it over his head. He tugged his shirt off, barely registering the rip. And then she was against him. Her breasts smashed to his chest. He reached up and cupped her from the side, his thumbs stroking her nipples. Palms on the counter, she arched back. He trailed kisses down, down, down to suckle her gently. She bucked against him, increasing the maddening pressure on his groin. He had to be inside her, already had a fumbling hand on the button of her jeans.

"What's... that?" she panted.

"Nothing," he mumbled around her nipple.

"No... oh... ah... yes!" Then, "Graham?"

"Hmm?"

"I think... that's my... oh, god..."

He lifted his head from her breast. Blinking, he tried to get a grasp on what she was trying to tell him. Then he heard it. He pulled his hand out of her pants and patted his pockets for his phone and then he remembered he'd left it in the car. "Not mine."

She unhooked her ankles and pushed at him to back up. He watched her jump down from the counter, her breasts bouncing as she ran to her purse. She rummaged around until she found her prize. It stopped ringing.

She frowned at the screen display. "My dad." She punched a couple of buttons and put the phone to her ear.

His gaze traveled from the crease between her brows to her naked torso. He wasn't gentleman enough to look away. And he couldn't summon up any guilt over it. She shoved a hand through her hair, lifting one breast. The one he'd been sucking on. Light red splotches dotted her skin where his beard had been. He liked that. He liked the flush in her cheeks and the way she looked bending over to pick up her bra and shirt. He tilted his head for a better look.

Clutching her clothes to her chest, she straightened. "What happened?"

His gaze snapped up to hers. Something in her tone...

"What does the doctor say?" That crease was back between her brows. "For how long?"

He moved to stand next to her.

"I'll be right there." She punched the phone off. "My aunt's at the hospital. I should go."

"What happened?"

She shoved her phone in the pocket of her jeans and began to dress. "She's had a really bad headache all day. Barely came out of her room." She struggled with the hook on her bra.

"Here, let me... there you go."

"Bet you hardly ever help a woman *into* her bra," she mumbled, missing his frown as she pulled her shirt over her head. Smoothing her hair back, she continued, "Mabel went to wake up my aunt for dinner only she couldn't. Auntie wouldn't wake up. Mabel called an ambulance." She stood for a moment, looking around as though she couldn't quite figure out what to do next.

"Do you want me to drive you?" he asked.

"To San Luis Obispo? That's over an hour away."

"I know how far it is."

"Why?"

"Why what?"

"Why do you want to drive me?"

The way she looked at him made the space between his shoulder blades itch. He wasn't sure what answer she was looking for, but he was pretty sure it would be the difference between him getting to see her breasts again or not.

"It's a long way," he said, wanting to spend more time with her.

"I know how far it is. I just told you."

"It's dark."

"Never mind."

He followed her as she wandered around, searching for something. "You shouldn't be alone."

"Ah, there they are." She pulled her shoes out from under the coffee table and sat down on the couch to put them on. "I said never mind."

"You don't make it easy to be nice to you."

"Put your shirt on, Graham."

"I'll put my shirt on and drive you to the hospital."

"Whatever."

He headed to the kitchen and found his shirt half hanging off one of the barstools. He pulled it on and noticed the top button was missing. "Damn." When he returned to the living room she wasn't there. "Erin?" He found her sitting on the edge of her bed, twisting a swatch of material. He eased down next to her.

"Auntie made me this."

"It's nice." Whatever it was.

"After my mom…left." She threaded the fabric back and forth between her hands. "Aunt Cerie was there. She moved in with my dad and me." She turned to him, her eyes wide and worried. "What if something happens to her?"

He wanted to tell her that everything would be all right. That good things happened to good people. Her aunt would be fine. And every other bullshit platitude. But he'd be lying. He knew from his experience in L.A. that bad things happened in spite of good intentions. Things were only ever 'all right' in fits and bursts. And that sometimes people died. Good people. In the place of some asshole who had that and more coming to him.

Instead he put a hand over hers, stilling their frantic worrying of the fabric. "I want to take you to the hospital. Let me."

She stared down at their joined hands. Her shoulders sagged as she let out a sigh ripe with relief. "Okay."

∼

THEY FOUND ERIN'S FATHER, Donald, pacing the hall outside her aunt's room. The fluorescent lights hollowed out Donald's cheeks and darkened the circles under his eyes. His hair stood up in white tufts around his head, which he plucked at randomly as he shuffled back and forth, mumbling to himself. Graham barely knew the man, but as they approached he could see that Donald wasn't well, probably hadn't been for some time.

"Dad." Erin rushed to her father.

Donald stopped his pacing and squinted at his daughter.

"Where's Auntie? And where are your glasses?"

Donald put a hand up to his temple. "Glasses?"

Graham hung back, watching the exchange that seemed all too familiar.

Erin's gaze wandered from the tips of her father's hair to his slippered feet. "Where are your shoes and jacket? It's freezing outside."

Rubbing his bare arms, Donald's brow creased. "Freezing."

Graham stepped forward with his jacket. "Here."

"Thank you." Erin took the jacket and bundled her father into it. "Better?"

Donald smoothed his hair back from his face.

"Where's Auntie? What do the doctors say?"

Donald blinked at Erin for a moment, then pointed to a door. Erin glanced back and forth between the door and her dad.

"I'll stay with him," Graham offered. "How about some coffee, Donald? I bet there's a machine in the waiting room." To Erin he said, "We'll wait for you in there."

"Thank you." She turned to go see her aunt.

Graham clapped Donald on the back. "How about that coffee?"

Donald followed alongside Graham. They found a machine in the waiting area that dribbled out weak-looking dredge. It tasted worse than it looked, but Graham drank it anyway. He sat in companionable silence with Donald, each of them absorbed in their thoughts.

Erin had mentioned her father's and aunt's troubles with their abilities, but the condition Donald was in had an eerie familiarity that made Graham think of his mother. He cast a look at Donald who sat staring into his untouched coffee, pulling at a tuft of hair over his ear. Graham reached over and lowered the man's hand. Donald looked at him with eyes the same color as Erin's and in their depths he saw an emptiness that cast chills over his skin. Would this happen to Erin?

Graham got up and looked down the hall. He'd promised Erin he'd stay with Donald, but all he wanted to do was go out and do something, anything that would bring all of this to an end. And he wanted Erin so bad he could hardly breathe when she was near.

He liked her too. She challenged him in ways he'd never been tested. She was different around him, more direct. She stood toe to toe with him and gave as good as she got. She was so freakin' beautiful, sometimes he had to blink twice just to make sure she was real. And someone or something was messing with her and her family.

Graham jammed his hands in his pockets and looked back at Donald. Maybe he'd know what was happening. He went to the man and sank back down in the chair next to him.

"Donald?"

Donald turned his head toward him with eyebrows raised.

"Do you know what's happening? To you? To Cerie?"

"Happening?" Donald looked at Graham, his gaze fixed and unfocused. But wait. Graham could see it. A spark. A fire burning deep and fierce.

No. Not vacant.

Trapped.

Trapped within his own mind.

*

Thank you for reading URGE! The next book in the LOVE STORIES series is RARE .

➤**CLICK HERE TO READ RARE**

If you enjoyed URGE, please consider leaving a review on your favorite book site. Reviews help readers find books!

➤URGE (A LOVE STORIES novel)

➤GOODREADS

Join my VIP Facebook group Babes with Books for

exclusive sneak peeks at my upcoming books & other, members only, perks:

➤www.facebook.com/groups/BabesWithBooks-ReaderGroup

Sign up to receive my newsletter for new release alerts, exclusive bonus content, and giveaways!

➤**www.bethyarnall.com/newsletter**

Turn the page to read an excerpt from RARE now!

EXCERPT FROM RARE

Erin sat at her aunt's bedside, holding the hand that had wiped her tears, braided her hair, and waved to her from their front porch everyday as she came home from school. She didn't know what she and her father would have done without Aunt Cerie. She'd come into their lives and everything that lay between Erin and her father had been put to rest.

Her parents' growing arguments had dotted Erin's days and nights with paralyzing dread, relieved only by bouts of guilt. She'd lie in her bed night after night, listening, knowing what was going to happen and unable to stop it. She'd *seen* it. Late one night, two months shy of her eighth birthday, Erin had awoken to the muffled sound of her parents' shouting. When the startling, terrifying silence came, she curled into a ball, squeezing her eyes shut. She knew her father was standing in the open doorway, watching her mother's taillights fade into the distance. He'd cried. Erin hadn't.

Aunt Cerie had arrived a few days later and had

never left. And now here she was in a hospital bed, her eyes jittering back and forth beneath her eyelids, her breath catching and hitching in her chest. She owed her aunt so much. Cerie let out a fretful sound, the kind a frightened child makes, and her hand jerked from Erin's. The alarm on the machine next to the bed suddenly went off, jolting Erin to her feet.

Erin did the only thing she could think of, she gripped Cerie's hand and reached out with her mind, not knowing if her aunt could hear her or not. *I'm here, Auntie. It's okay. I'm right here. Everything's going to be all right.*

After a moment, Cerie settled in the bed, but her eyes still darted back and forth beneath her eyelids.

A frazzled-looking nurse bustled in and pressed a few buttons, putting an end to the noise of the machine. She flipped through papers on a clipboard. "Looks like we'll have to increase her dosage," she said.

"Dosage of what? What's wrong with my aunt?" Erin asked, trying to keep the fear from her voice.

"I'll send the doctor in to talk with you. He's just finishing up with another patient."

"Thank you."

"Are you okay?" The nurse asked, pointing to her own nose. "You're bleeding."

Startled, Erin touched a finger to her nostril and it came away red. It was getting worse.

"Here." She handed Erin a box of tissues. "You better sit down. Apply pressure. Don't tilt your head back."

Erin did as instructed. "Thank you," she mumbled around a wad of tissues.

"I'll send the doctor in to speak with you shortly."

Erin continued her silent ramblings, which seemed to soothe Cerie considerably. She wasn't as agitated as she'd been when Erin first arrived. Erin focused her thoughts, keeping them positive. After a few moments, her nose stopped bleeding so she went into the bathroom to clean up. When she came out, a doctor was at her aunt's bedside, listening to her chest.

He looked up as Erin came into the room. "Hello. I'm Doctor Frost." He took the stethoscope out of his ears and slung it around his neck, then gently raised Cerie's eyelids, shining a light back and forth.

"I'm her niece, Erin."

"Can you tell me about what's been happening with your aunt?"

What could Erin say? That her aunt was a mind reader? That someone was messing with her ability? All of their abilities. That her aunt didn't have the same defenses as she and her father and that's why she was so affected? "She's been having severe head pain off and on."

"When she came in, she was nonresponsive." He flipped up the blanket covering Cerie's feet, took out a wheelie thing and rolled it over her the contours of her foot. "She's not responding to pain. Has she had an accident? Maybe a fall?"

"No, not that I know of."

"Is she on any medication, prescription or otherwise?"

"No. Absolutely not."

"Does she have a history of migraines or high blood pressure? Seizures? Mental disorders?"

"No. None of those. She's always been healthy."

The doctor felt her aunt's scalp, her neck. "No signs of trauma. I want to run some tests. Mostly neuro-logical."

Erin didn't ask what the doctor was looking for. There was nothing in this hospital that could help her aunt. "Is she...suffering?"

He straightened and looked at Erin. "We've got her under sedation. She was quite agitated when she first arrived."

"But is she in any pain?"

"To be honest, I'm not sure. She's not responding to the medication as she should, so I've prescribed a higher dose sedative. I'm concerned about her heart. Is there a history in your family of heart disease or high blood pressure?"

"No. What's wrong with her heart?"

"Her blood pressure is elevated. We've given her some medication to help bring it down, but again, it isn't having the effect it should. Can you think of anything that could have caused this? Any changes in her life or lifestyle?"

"Sorry. No."

He nodded and consulted the chart he held in his hand. He scribbled down some notes, then flipped it shut and headed for the door. "We'll keep a close eye on your aunt."

"Thank you." Erin watched the doctor leave, then

turned to her aunt. "You've got to calm down, Auntie. You heard the doctor." She slipped Cerie's hand into her own. "I don't know what's happening to you... to us, but I'm going to find out."

Her aunt shifted in the bed.

"Graham's here. He knows, Auntie. He knows all about my ability. I'm helping him find out what's happening."

Cerie's body stiffened and her heart rate went wild on the monitor.

"Auntie, please calm down. It's all right. Everything's going to be okay." Erin flicked a nervous glance from her aunt to the monitor and back again. She didn't know what she'd do without her aunt. Worry crawled inside her and weaved its web, wrapping her chest in tight bands. Erin couldn't lose her. She wouldn't lose her. She'd do whatever it took to stop whoever was doing this to them. Whatever it took.

Graham stared into Donald's eyes, chilled by what he saw. Donald was there, but inaccessible, as though he was looking at Graham from the bottom of a deep, dark pit.

"Tell me what's happening to you," Graham said.

Donald's gaze held firm as though he was trying to convey something he couldn't with words. "Happening," he repeated.

"He won't tell you anything," a voice said from behind him. Graham spun around to see Mabel, standing in the doorway. She made her way toward them, her eyes on Donald. There was a softness in the look she gave him and an extra sway in her step. "He hasn't been able to do much more than repeat words or phrases for days now." She settled into the chair next to Donald and patted his shoulder.

"What are you doing here?" Graham asked.

Mabel smoothed the hair that Donald had plucked at back down over his ear. "Erin and I have been taking turns looking after Donald and Cerie." She turned her cunning gaze on Graham, brows raised. "I could ask you the same question, Sheriff."

"What do you make of Donald's and Cerie's...conditions?" he asked, avoiding Mabel's question, at the same time, feeling disrespectful talking about Donald as if he weren't sitting inches away.

"I think..." She stopped Donald from reaching up to pull at his hair again and twined his fingers in hers. "They're in trouble."

Graham had to tread carefully here, unsure how much Mabel knew about the December family's abilities especially Erin's. "How so?"

"Isn't it obvious?" She leaned across Donald and whispered, "Evil's taken up residence in San Rey."

"What do you mean, evil?"

"Witches," she breathed.

"Witches." He pressed his lips flat to keep from laughing out loud. *Was she serious?*

"It's the only explanation. They've put a spell on San Rey. All the crimes...the murder...you can't tell me that's not the work of sinister beings."

Graham sat back in his chair. She was dead serious. Witches. "Is that why half the town has horse shoes tacked to their front doors?"

"Witch repellant."

"Well, it's not working. And just how did the town come to believe witches are causing all the problems?"

Mabel's gaze slunk to the corner of the room. "Everyone knows Samhain is their high holiday."

"Mabel," he began to admonish, then decided against it. Let the town's people believe what they wanted. It wasn't like he had a better explanation for what was happening. "You haven't seen the witches, have you?"

She scooted to the edge of her chair, her full focus back on Graham. "As a matter of fact—"

*

Want to read more?

➤One-click RARE Now➤

★A 2016 Daphne du Maurier contest winner★

If you loved URGE, you'll love the sexy, funny, award nominated INNOCENT serial. Cora's brother was convicted of a murder he didn't commit and it's up to her to set him free. Inspired by real cases taken on by The Innocence Project.

★ Nominated in 2017 for the Romance Writers of America Rita® award★

➤One-click EPISODE ONE Now➤

Looking for something lighter and funny? Check out THE MISADVENTURES OF MAGGIE MAE series, starting with WAKE UP, MAGGIE, available now! Maggie has to keep her very inappropriate thoughts to herself about the FBI Special Agent assigned to protect her from a murderer.

➤One-click WAKE UP, MAGGIE Now➤

ALSO BY BETH YARNALL

The Misadventures of Maggie Mae

Wake Up, Maggie

You're Mine, Maggie

Find Me, Maggie

Azalea March Mysteries

Dyed and Gone

Beth Writing as Betty Paper

Exposed

Captive

Tinsel

Piano Lessons

ABOUT THE AUTHOR

USA Today best selling author and Rita® finalist, Beth Yarnall, writes mysteries, romantic suspense, and the occasional hilarious tweet. She lives in Southern California with her husband, two sons, and their rescue dogs where she is hard at work on her next novel. For more information about Beth and her novels please visit her website- www.bethyarnall.com

facebook.com/bethyarnallauthor

amazon.com/author/bethyarnall

bookbub.com/authors/beth-yarnall

BETH'S BOOKS FOR WRITERS

Crafting Unputdownable Fiction series

Going Deep Into Deep Point of View

Making Description Work Hard For You

Some Like It Hot: Writing Sex and Romance